REPLICATED

Offering New Flavors *in Fiction*

A Cybil Lewis Novella

Nicole Givens Kurtz

Mocha Memoirs Press, LLC
Winston-Salem, NC

CONTENTS

ISBN: 978-0-9998522-1-7

Replicated: A Cybil Lewis Novella

Copyright © 2016 Nicole Givens Kurtz

Edited by Melissa Gilbert at ClickingKeys.com

Cover design by Nicole Kurtz

Published by

Mocha Memoirs Press

931 S. Main Street

Ste. B-143

Kernersville, NC 27284

Mochamemoirspress.com

Providing New Flavors in Fiction!

replicate-[rep-li-keyt] - repeat, duplicate, or reproduce, especially for experimental purposes.

CHAPTER 1

MONDAY AROUND NOON, I landed my wauto, a wind automobile, in front of my office building, a square hulk structure with dark windows that offered views over the impoverished, the depraved, and the former capitol building. With the United States divided into a series of territories and pieces, the D.C. territory, commonly called the District, had become an entity unto itself. What was once shared within a unified country became a grab all for territories in proximity to the goodies. So in a blink, the District became a looming presence in the territories' puzzle pieces. Some sections befriended the District; others sought ways to defend themselves against us.

Trust didn't exist between the territories. Think of it as a bunch of young siblings whose parents had died unexpectedly in an accident. There's no one to watch, correct, or punish their behavior—in seconds, everything burst into scrapes, squabbles, and screeching. The drawn lines on the map weren't invisible. People physically felt them as they crossed over from one to the other. The culture, the regulations, and the cities' textures varied.

My office sat nestled in the sector filled with mixed use structures and war-weary residents. The area had long since been discarded by more prominent people.

The lobby doors parted to reveal Jane, my inspector-in-training, at her desk, typing—well, pecking—away on her report for a client who had hired us to document—with graphics for her attorney and court proceedings—all of her husband's comings and goings. Not for a divorce. She wanted the JPEGs to have him committed to a mental institution. Seems the husband's fetish for robot parts had finally forced her to take some action.

Why trust such a secret to me?

Because I keep things *private*. I'm Cybil Lewis, private inspector and all around busy body about the District.

"Morning." I lifted my satchel over my head from where I'd strapped it across my torso.

"More like afternoon." Jane paused, quirked an eyebrow at me then returned to her search and find activity with the keyboard.

I headed straight for the coffeemaker. It had its own space, an alcove of caffeine heaven. No sooner had I put my mug down and it delivered the hot beverage did the lobby doors open for a second time.

From behind me, I heard Jane call out. "Hey! Stop!"

With my hand on the lasergun, I rolled out of the coffee alcove and directly into the lobby proper. Across from me, a man had almost reached the door to my private, inner office, having bypassed the receptionist's desk and Jane.

"Where is Cybil Lewis?" he demanded over his shoulder.

"Be careful who you ask for." I didn't bother smiling, my lasergun trained on him.

I couldn't have smiled for long anyway. Standing with his hands casually shoved into his uniform pockets stood a blast from my past I'd rather have left in the history books.

He turned to face me.

Benjamin Satou.

From the corner of my eye, I saw Jane scowl in confusion. She'd moved from her desk beside the coffee alcove and come to stand just behind me.

"You look you've seen a ghost." She spoke low as we're trained to do.

"She wasn't here before," Satou said.

"Jane, Private Satou. Private Satou, Jane, my inspector-in-training."

"Yeah, I don't care who you are. Get out!" Jane placed her hand at the small of her back. To the common onlooker, it seemed as if she simply rubbed a lower back ache, but I knew her knife resided in a special holder.

We didn't take kindly to people barging into our office. Benjamin set his feet like he meant to make us remove him.

"Jane," I cautioned. She didn't know that taking on Satou would be a mistake.

She paused, but she didn't like it. "He can't just come in here, demanding..." Jane didn't take her eyes off of him as she spoke to me.

"Just leave it, for now." I heard every word, but it ended up coming through as a hazy buzzing. Her instincts didn't lie. The potential for danger increased the moment he stepped into the lobby.

The real issue stood about six feet two inches in glossy ebony military boots. I noticed that he stood nearly as tall as me at five feet, eleven inches. A shimmering one-piece uniform skimmed a muscled body—slender, but toned tight. Not even the military's lined and layered uni-can kept me from scoping out those details of his body.

Normally, I would've been more impressed by such a nice package, but nothing had ever been normal—or nice—about Satou. Plus, I'd seen it before.

"Miss Lewis, we meet again." Satou's mouth twitched at the end of my last name. His brown eyes, rimmed with scarlet, peered out from beneath the fall of raven bangs. "You're surprised that me being here hurts. It hurts right here."

He touched his chest where a heart should've been.

"Cyborgs don't feel, Satou." I hated robots and the jury was still out on how I felt about people and robotic parts being combined. "So save that programmed bull for your engineers."

"Cyborg?" Jane said the word like it tasted bad in her mouth. She inched backward, her body rigid and jerky in its movements. "Against regulations here, in the District. Who the hell *are* you?"

"Private Benjamin Satou. Cyborg. Secret military weapon."

"Former client," he added and tried to grin. It just made Jane scowl harder.

"You and I are going to stay history." I didn't move, but the cold steadiness filtered over me. Familiar. When my honey and kindness ebbed out, icy indifference ebbed in.

"Don't be that way." He tried again to smile, but his facial muscles didn't seem to want to cooperate.

"How's the wife?"

He frowned at that. His lips tugged downward in disapproval.

"Deceased," he answered.

Jane watched our interchange, but she inched wider out, putting him at the point of the triangle we now formed.

"Why does a cyborg need a private inspector?" Jane crouched, ready to strike.

Benjamin attempted to smile. It looked as natural as the ones airbrushed on mannequins.

"What do you want this time?" I seconded, my hand tightening around my lasergun's grip. Instantly calmer, I tried a smile of my own. Look at me—doing polite.

Jane cast me a glance, but I ignored her unspoken question. Snared by curiosity, I lowered the gun a little.

"You were so helpful the last time I purchased your services, and I need them again." Benjamin rotated his neck, popping it as if the wires had kinked up together.

"The last time I helped you, your wife ended up dead." I could still hear Charlotte's cybernetic body hissing and clicking as she engaged Benjamin in battle.

"That wasn't my fault." He had the programming to at least act like it bothered him.

Last time, he followed me to his missing wife. Their reunited pairing came to blows and overall fighting. The EuroRepublic had kidnapped Charlotte Satou, changed her into a cyborg, and set her on a collision course to destroy the District's sole—according to Satou—equivalent. I left before I could see the turnout of the fight, but now that Benjamin stood in the center of my lobby, I could figure out who won that battle.

No inspection necessary.

"Depends on who you ask." I didn't move from my spot. Just because we had history didn't mean I trusted him.

The faint whirling and clicks of machinery ran across my nerves, making me restless. I fought it. Any sudden moves might invoke some combatant response from Satou. Robots. Couldn't trust them as far as you programmed them. I noticed that Satou's language software had been upgraded. Years ago he'd been a rough hodgepodge of parts and programmable nanos. Now, he'd been worked over with smooth speech patterns and slicker movements, not the hurky-jerky hothead soldier from before.

Time heals all, and well, so does better tech.

"Surely, you know where your wife is. Some cleaner parts in the north maybe?" I holstered the gun. I didn't want to wear out my arm.

His grin wilted. Cold eyes shifted from Jane before rolling to me.

"Your job in the war is to kill people. My job is to decide which jobs I want to take. Listening helps me do that. So comply by answering the questions." I gave him an it's-your-lucky-day smile to take the edge off my words.

"Yes. Right." With a thick sigh, he strolled over to the lobby's visitor chairs and sat down in one. He got up again and began pacing. Long, thin legs stalked the length of the wall, bypassing my holographic image of landscapes. He paced about the space as if he couldn't relax. "Regulator Tom said you were the best P.I. in the entire district."

Daniel Tom wouldn't ever say I was the best. He'd eat his cigarette first.

"The EuroRepublic…" Satou either halted his answer or his cybernetic program didn't allow for that information to be shared.

"War's over. Go home. We got better things to do!" Jane shouted from her new position by her desk.

Benjamin Satou cleared his throat. He looked at me, but answered Jane. "I can't."

"Listen, you swore allegiance and gave your blood to the District. Cosmic Fate doesn't give a damn about individuality, just like the DC Army. You're a number. War's all done. Those numbers get erased." I shrugged to punctuate my words.

Benjamin grinned and a blanket of cold clammy sweat erupted over my body. The smile failed to inspire warmth or even reassurance.

"Regulator Tom said you were difficult, and that you'd enlisted at sixteen."

"Yeah, well, he would know," I quipped.

Satou sat down again before rising back up. "I don't like closed in spaces. I remember this office being bigger."

"The only thing's that changed since your last visit is you." I softened my tone. PTSD affected everyone differently, even cyborgs. "You got to see the A.I.s?"

"Your retainer's 1700 District dollars, right?" He asked instead of answering my question.

"No deal. Go home." My voice turned hard, but I meant it when I said it.

"Yes ma'am." Benjamin fought down a frustrated sob. Voice wobbly and eyes tearing, he did manage to hold my gaze without melting. Silence hung between us as tangible as wet wool. I wanted him to leave, but something, maybe loneliness, kept him hovering in my presence.

"I'm doing my best." Benjamin's shoulders slouched and his eyes remained fixated on the carpet. "I can't live without her. For years the war blotted out the hole, the ache in here. When that ended, field work, and special missions kept me busy, but now there's nothing but this ugly quiet."

"When the winds of change blow, it's more cyclone than gentle breeze." I sipped from my mug, my coffee lukewarm.

"You don't get it." Benjamin's voice ached in its passion. Eyes gleaming, he continued. "I've been discontinued. Honorable discharge and now that Charlotte's gone, I don't know what to do."

"What?" Numbness flattened my words against the forced heat blowing gently through the room.

He didn't sit down and his hands didn't stay still. They roamed about his thighs, through his hair, and on the chair in front of him. Although the war had ended years ago, Satou acted like it had ended yesterday.

He met my eyes, but those blue orbs seemed quite unfocused as if he wasn't looking so much at me as through me. He didn't seem to be in a great mood. After all, his entire purpose had been obliterated. How could you be in a great mood after something like that? Was another episode of violence about to erupt from Mount Solider? A part of me courted the urge to push him just a teeny tiny bit, just to see if I was right.

"Are you sure you weren't kicked out?" I had to ask that question before I wasted my time.

"I received an honorable discharge." He blew out his simmering temper as he swung around toward me, body rigid with rage. "How could they just discharge me? Not me! I'm a lethal weapon!"

Before I could breathe, the lasergun took residence up in my fist for the second time. Pointed directly into the face of the fast blowing and now apologizing soldier, the weapon didn't waver.

"I'm sorry. I'm sorry." He waved his hands in surrender, in slow, deliberate circles. "I...I get angry sometimes. I mean you no harm, Miss Lewis, you know me."

A smear of blue jeans and black flashed across the room. Jane's blade caught the overhead lights and gleamed against his throat's creamy texture. He became very still. He hadn't see her move.

Yes, Jane moved that fast.

"Yeah, but I don't." She pressed the knife to his throat and it bit into his skin or celluloid. "So, we ain't got all night. Whatever the hell you want, speak it plain."

Her patience had been exhausted. A recently lit cigarette dangled precariously from her full lips. She didn't remove it, but if need be, she could slice off Satou's weapon straight from his shoulders without uttering another word.

Yeah, she was that good.

I put my focus back on Satou.

"Another eruption will cost you blood or oil or whatever cyborgs spill." Jane released him with a slight shove.

"You understand, I've gotta know. Years of having my ass blown to bits, watching comrades burst and blown into pieces, death ravaging all I held dear, except for, for Char. I—I survived because of her. Now that's she dead..."

He broke off.

So much emotion for a robot. Something bothered me about the whole routine, but I couldn't place it right off. Satou hadn't told me why he had come here, only bemoaned the death of his wife—by his hands. He could have survivor's guilt. Seemed unlikely since he had been the cause of Charlotte's demise.

"I've been a private inspector for a long time," I warned, letting the ice in my voice slice through his fog of emotional turmoil. "Prepare yourself for life with non-violent human beings. You've been out of the service for how long?"

"Two months," he croaked.

"That's a lifetime to some." I spoke slow and clear. He had to hear this to keep his sanity. "A blink of an eye to others. I'm not sure why you're here, but know this, some things are best left alone."

The emancipated soldier swept his eyes over to me. Steady, they latched onto mine, and for a brief second I wondered if he'd told me all of it. A serious keen intelligence shot out from those eyes.

I'd been hoodwinked by Satou before.

Fool me once; shame on you. Fool me twice...well, I might shoot you.

"I just thought you could help." He shrugged.

Something in his voice snatched my attention back to his face.

"Have you gone to the shrinks?"

"No."

No wonder he tried to take my head off. Without the head shrinking and the merry meds combo, readjusting back into everyday life in the quadrant meant aggressive outbursts, violence, and moods that swung faster than the current governor's tax promises. Used to fighting and the manufactured chaos of war, Satou wouldn't do well with the silent, peaceful, mundane life spelled out in the District's many sectors. This soldier hadn't fought off post-traumatic stress with the normal remedies. It equated him to a walking bomb.

All things I needed to know before I engaged him.

If you poke a sleeping tiger...

Sighing with regret, but trying hard to conjure some honey to help sweeten this situation, I looked at Jane. She shrugged as if to say it was my show.

My grandmother used to say that everyone had a certain level of honey in their systems. She continued by saying I had an over-abundance of vinegar, but hey, on the rare days I got a potential client, I could do sweet, kind, and nice—everything to draw the client in.

Today had me elbow-deep in the hive. My attempts to be nice cost me a lot of tart replies and time, moments I'd never be able to retrieve again.

Jane rotated her index finger around her temple.

My gut agreed. Satou was nuts. What he needed, I couldn't provide. Hell, I couldn't even provide it for myself—peace.

"I'm sorry." I put up my gun.

His head snapped eyes bulging, hands rolled into fists. "You're not sorry!"

All manner of alarm coursed through me. I waved Jane back, but I didn't know if that strategy would hold water. Cyborgs did not respond to death the way humans did, but the human inside Satou acted like he wanted to die anyway. As lethal as Jane was, Satou may have been deadlier still.

"I used to be in the District's army. What you're looking for, I can't give you. Finding people, things—that I can do. Helping you find peace is beyond my skillset."

"Just tell me what to do. What I do about *this*?" he managed around a hard swallow. He clasped his hands in front of him and hunched over, threatening to ball up into misery.

"This is living. When you've spent so much time killing, it's hard to see the benefits of surviving, of life." I knew firsthand Satou's struggle. Most warriors did. Well, the ones who held onto those last strips of humanity.

Benjamin coughed out his emotional lump. He didn't break down into tears. Whether because cyborgs didn't cry or because soldiers didn't, I wasn't sure.

"Listen, you're suffering from the aftershocks of carnage. Go see the head-shrinkers and the A.I.s. Take your meds. Get better." I crossed my arms.

He stood, and with a sober look back at me, turned, and left.

There was something intriguing about him, strange, in a way that made me want to investigate him. Nothing sneaky, per se, just something *off*. What I didn't need in my life, I reminded myself, was a client who was *off*. The Irving case wasn't too long ago, and to tell the truth, a sour lump languished over me. Getting caught up in a major *anything* didn't sound even remotely appealing—and no, I didn't care how much it paid.

As soon as the office doors hushed closed, Jane swiveled her chair to face me. With a wide grin, she watched me. That smirk looked like a lot of trouble, crowded with mischief.

"You sure got some reputation." Her knife had already vanished into its hiding spot on her person. "Everybody wanna meet you— shake your hand..."

I waved her off with a laugh. Although my coffee had become room temperature, I drank it down. Even something lukewarm could chase the cold chills from my flesh. Satou had resurrected far too many memories—ones I had long since buried.

"So, what did you do to get kicked out of the army?" she inquired, a flutter of amusement around her words. "Must've been bad. Normally, the only way out is in a body bag."

"Those wounds are still fresh. Let's leave them to heal." I headed toward my private office.

"It's been what? Twelve years?"

"I'm ignoring you."

"Eliminating mental photos to save yourself from your past doesn't help anyone," Jane advised.

"Oh no, don't start the *I'm a therapist* role."

"I'm just being real. You had all that advice for the cyborg. Heal thyself."

"And I'm gone."

I retreated to my private office to escape Jane's pseudo-shrink. Once she got started, she wouldn't stop until I cried or confessed my darkest secrets. Since I didn't cry, it would be secrets, and I had far too many of those.

The topic of secrets led me back to Satou.

Clearly, the man had lost what he could not hold.

CHAPTER 2

IT WAS a little after midnight when I finally stepped into my gloomy but sparkling clean apartment. I removed the ponytail tie, and my shoulder-length braids crashed down to my shoulders. The satchel smacked the floor in the kitchen where the carpet ended and the linoleum began. It held little but a refrigerator, a slender gray stove, and a coffeemaker, but it was only me who lived here. Wheezing and pushing out infrequent puffs of air, the complex's air conditioning once again seemed to be on its last, wobbly legs. No doubt it would kill off in the wee hours of the morning, threatening me to sleep in the shower with the water on cold.

Thank goodness the fridge worked well. I pulled out a cold bottle of Peck beer, twisted off the top, and drank. Something had to keep me from melting.

I walked over to the sofa and plopped down. In thirteen minutes, Bruce Lee was going to be on screen kicking the crap out of all evil-doers. Fatigued from a day at the office, I took off my shoes and clicked on the telemonitor with one goal: watching until I drooled into my beer for the next hour while my body decompressed the day.

First, though, I wanted a shower. Not only to wash off the slimy feeling of sweat, but to rid the nagging feeling that I'd missed some-thing about Satou today. Something significant. My gut churned in warning. I replayed the exchanges over and over in my head. The nagging remained consistent. I'd missed something.

Minutes later, I dragged myself out of the shower after cleaning up and rinsing off. Film and beer. That's all I wanted right then and there. No more thinking about anything for fear my head would explode.

After two hours, approximately one movie, just when I thought I was home free and relaxed, my telemonitor dinged. The large, white screen halted all shots of Bruce doing his best to act and kick butt. In burning black font, the words "incoming communication" blinked.

The Fates weren't in the mood for being kind this night.

I clicked the viewer and there stood D.C. Regulator Daniel Tom, his grim face taking up a fourth of the camera. His light brown eyes seemed to sag and a nearly finished cigarette already dangled from his lips.

Without wasting any more time, I answered. "Daniel."

"Lewis, I need you to get out here." His voice battled against the wind. The cigarette threatened to breakaway despite Daniel's tight clenched teeth's hold.

My eyebrows rose in question. "How come you can't remember that I'm not a regulator anymore?"

He glared at me. "Those pretty dark eyes don't scare me. Come down here, anyway. It's that soldier from a few years back. Sowers, Sanders..."

"Satou," I finished, my heart speeding up its thump-one, thump-two routine.

"Yeah. Him." Daniel removed his cigarette, blew a stream of smoke, and then dropped it out of the camera's sight.

"Where?"

"Yeah, I'm getting to it. I'm at the, uh, which one is this? Yeah, yeah, okay. I'm at the West Potomac Park."

"Be there in a few." I stood up with a groan of regret, not trying to hide my displeasure from him.

"Don't rush. Take your time." He stuffed a fresh, unlit cigarette into his mouth. "We'll be here awhile. It's a goddamn mess."

With that cheery bit, he disconnected the feed.

I downloaded the attached coordinates. Daniel's comment about him not going anywhere meant a possible long night for me, though it had been weeks since Daniel and I worked a case. The memories remained. I already felt exhausted.

What had Satou done?

———

I reached the park within twenty minutes or so, thanks to good flying and lack of traffic. Daniel waved me through the yellow caution beam and by a big boulder of a regulator. He glowered at me. A civilian—hell, a PI—at a regulations scene.

Scary!

"See that box over there? That's our problem." Daniel neglected to say hello or bother with any pleasantries. He gestured to a large, square box in the grass at the river's edge where vioTechs processed the scene all around it. Buzzing about with gloved hands, scanners, and recording devices.

Yet no one touched it.

"Who found it?"

Daniel searched his tablet. A slight wrinkle creased his forehead.

I studied him as he searched his notes. Some would consider Daniel handsome, but not many. Strange, but most hatchlings had been considered perfect, but I doubted anyone on the force knew. Unlike some hatchlings—artificially created humans—Daniel took great pains to hide his tattoo, even resulting to covering it with body makeup.

Don't tell him that I told you.

"A fisherman found the cardboard box at the edge of the river. Nerves of steel."

"How so?" I coughed out the reeking odor of fish and spoiled water that rose from the container like a tight fist, slamming through my usual violation scene cool.

"Hell, I wouldn't fish in this shit," he said with a completely indifferent expression on his face. Daniel had finished his cigarette long before I arrived at the violation scene, but the scent lingered on his regulator uniform, underscoring the stench from the box.

"What's in the box? Satou?" I asked.

"Lewis, today's Christmas." Daniel headed back to the box that had been moved onto a levitating gurney. "A present. Don't say I ain't never given you anything."

"You haven't looked yet?" I asked, slightly surprised and wondering why I didn't just keep my own mouth shut. "You're full of..."

"Give it a looksee." Daniel nodded in its direction.

The soggy flaps had already been pulled back. Scales, algae, and mud stuck to it like the horrendous smell of waste. I fought back my gag reflex—too many men around to go barfing up beer. It was difficult enough that Daniel knew I slept in pink pajamas on occasion. My reputation was on the line and depended on if I threw up now or held it until I got home.

Stupid, I know, but I did have something to prove.

The smell alone made my stomach rumble with queasiness.

It was way too early in the morning for this shit.

But Daniel expected nothing less than my full one hundred and fifteen percent.

Call it tradition.

We go back a long way. Daniel and I had both worked for the District's army some time ago. Consistently, he and I ended up being first and second place in all areas of boot camp training. Sometimes he'd win; sometimes I'd kick his butt. After a while of hating each other and viewing the other as solely a rival, we forged a friendship steeped in trust, loyalty, and competition.

We split after boot camp. Daniel went his way and I went mine. Yet it was Daniel who stood by me during my sexual harassment hearing, and it was Daniel who testified on my behalf, thus saving me from serious reprimand. The District's army meant business. We still competed, of course, and the competitive knot that tied us together had never faltered.

Which was why I put on such a courageous mask.

"You all right, Lewis?" Daniel leered around a freshly lit cigarette.

It sounded like he had a chuckle in his throat.

Screw him.

"Better than your wife," I retorted while peering around the box for clues as to what may lay inside.

The pack of regulators roared in laughter. Daniel scowled, for his wife had left him months ago. Low blow, but he asked for it.

Taking a steadying breath, I looked inside the box—feeling ever more like Pandora. Something horrid resided inside there. I just knew it. Kind of like when you know you aren't going to like that lima bean soup. You just know.

Christmas this wasn't.

The vioTechs had collected everything, if there was anything to begin with beyond the item itself. So, I took a deep breath, let it out, and held the next one as I looked inside, leaning over it to see inside its smelly depths.

There—inside a plastic bag—was a human torso, sans head, arms, and legs. They'd been removed, rather expertly. No hesitation marks, no practice slices. The naked chest still had dark curls scattered around it like random flowers, sprouting around the flat nipples. Scorching existed around the places where the limbs should have been. Laser.

"ID chip?" I croaked, throat dry, words squeaking around the lump lodged inside my esophagus.

"No." Daniel shook his head as he read something on his tablet.

I stared down at the makeshift coffin and clenched my teeth against the smell.

My feet glided as if they had a mind of their own and knew that this wasn't the place to be. Daniel's hand gently stopped me from walking away. His hand steadied me, and for once, I was glad he was there, despite his initial jeering.

"DNA scanner identified him as Benjamin Satou. What's left of him."

I shoved my trembling hands into my pants pockets, and tried to sip in sweeter smelling air as I turned away.

"Daniel, that can't be him. I just saw him earlier today. That box, that torso, looked like it'd been in the water for some time."

The decomposed torso had been gray, bloated, and water worn. The skin slipped in areas not charred by laser slice marks.

Daniel blew a stream of smoke from the corner of his mouth. "DNA scans said it's him."

"It's wrong."

My voice sounded absent of emotion—hollow—like a damn robot. With each horrid act I witnessed, a piece of my humanity died, or so I have been told. I'd be totally desensitized by the age of forty.

"DNA doesn't lie, Lewis."

"No, but the scanner can be manipulated. That's not him. I tell you what though, there's one sick puppy running around the District. Maybe even leading the pack."

This was well beyond the realm of what people did to each other. Daniel's hand on my shoulder suddenly felt like it weighed a ton. The desire to flee, to hurry like a hurricane, blossomed again in my mind. I squashed it with an annoyed sigh and one long glance back at Daniel.

"We can't use anything else to ID him, so until we get something more, it's Benjamin Satou."

"Whoever did this had time and privacy."

"And?" Daniel said, his breath a thin whisper across my neck.

"Damn it, Daniel," I said, low enough for only his ears to hear. "This isn't a quiz!"

"All I got is a box with a torso that's ident-DNA-fied to Benjamin

Satou, who according to his wauto's GPS coordinates, came to your office."

"So, you got nothing." I gazed at the box. "'Cause that ain't him."

He sighed and came around to face me with a small smile on his face. He looked exhausted. "What can you tell me about his visit?"

I gave him the one finger salute. "You know I don't talk client business with regs."

"So you're working for him?" Daniel went on as if I hadn't said anything.

"No, I don't work for him, but I have worked for him in the past."

"Tell me something I don't already know." He grunted at me, his eyes on his tablet. "It's gonna be a damn mess. I give it another ten minutes and the army's going to be marching in to take over this thing."

"Are you listening?"

"Yeah. I'm hearing the same thing I always hear from you —whining."

"The next time you call me for an assist, you're going to get a big fat fuck no."

We'd reached an impasse. My gut told me that the torso shoved into that box didn't belong to Benjamin Satou, despite what the DNA scanner said. If it wasn't Satou then who was it? Who would do this?

Daniel glanced up at me, his eyes only, not his head. "Did it occur to you that maybe the person who came to see you wasn't Benjamin Satou?"

With my patience spent, I started for my wauto, but stopped at his words. I turned to him. "I know what he looks like, hell Daniel, you sent him to me. The person in my office was Satou. The details in the conversation and memories he shared, all of it had been authentic and accurate."

"You scanned him?" Daniel coughed.

I glared.

"Didn't think so." He smiled with an expression that was a veiled as a virgin bride on her wedding day.

He had a point. Damn him.

After what happened with a previous client changing his face, I knew Daniel's suggestion didn't lie outside the realm of possibility or plastic surgery.

"Then why have my coordinates in his wauto?"

Daniel shrugged. "Dunno. That's one of many questions."

"And why here?"

A fly-by over water, through parks and memorials, wasn't uncommon. Waterfront parks and the marina were close to every major flight path through the District. Hell, anyone could've dumped the box from their boat, ship, or craft, nothing to it. They'd be in violation of the park space regulation, but the force fields only went so far up.

A huddle of people at the park packed the area behind the beam. Eager faces and those chatting on their personal telemonitors created a buzz. Most were dressed in shorts and tee shirts, sunglasses and flip-flops. Each trying to catch a glimpse of the scene and human malice at its finest.

Nothing united folks like death and murder.

I left the scene, ducking under the yellow caution beam. I wanted to slap Daniel, hard across his face for bringing me down here, but that wouldn't help alleviate my dilemma.

Was it Benjamin Satou in the box? If so, where the hell was the rest of him?

Once I reached my wauto, I got in with my mind made up. I let out the breath I had forgotten. A torso—sans limbs and head. Horrid. No one deserved that kind of exit. I shuddered involuntarily.

Where did the rest of Satou go? Why had he been killed in this way?

Already a ball of stress tightened at the base of my neck.

Whoever was in the cardboard box didn't die easily. The cut

marks were clean, as if the killer didn't give a rat's ass that the person had been a human being.

Or alive.

Cold. Detached. Smart.

Daniel definitely was dealing with a botched human being— one with a gigantic hole were his conscience should've been.

CHAPTER 3

WITHOUT STOPPING to think about it anymore, I set the autopilot and switched on Bach. Already well into Tuesday morning, I cranked the wind channel up to four. Cool breezes blew my budding stress right into the back seat, through the trunk vents, and beyond. I pictured my stress as tiny suctioned cup fiends going splat against the windshields of those flying behind me.

Sometimes I had so many things cooking on the backburner my mental kitchen caught fire.

Leaving me burned.

My telemonitor dinged and I answered, feeling the Fates fail me yet again. I did so without checking the viewer first, in anticipation of something or someone important.

It wasn't.

I should have known better.

The slow connection stalled the video feed so the audio came through first.

"What do you want this time, Daniel?" I asked, my eyes on the review mirror as I changed lanes.

"Good morning, Cybil." A male voice cajoled right before the blotchy pixel feed cleared up.

And it wasn't Daniel's.

Trey.

Ex-boyfriend. Territory Alliance agent. Hatchling.

Yeah, he was a hatchling. Sperm. Egg. Stir. Incubate. Human.

It had been two weeks since I walked out on Trey and a great delicious T-bone steak. We'd gone to dinner and like all the times we tried to reconnect, after our break-up, it all fell apart in a matter of hours. Our break-up bruise continued to be tender, even now.

For both of us.

The full body view served as great eye candy. I knew he was off duty because he wore a crimson tee-shirt and ebony jeans. Not to be outdone, he also wore black sneakers with red letter A on the side. His tailored suit must be at the cleaners.

Didn't he know it was sweltering outside? Maybe he wasn't in my territory.

"What do you want?" It sounded casual and cool, as if I wasn't dying to tear into him.

"I'm working a case. Aren't you?" He didn't look into the camera, but rather down at the tablet in his hands.

When I didn't answer, he slowly raised his gray eyes to mine.

"Ah, yes, you've talked to the regulators." He smiled, an uneasy, unsure one.

Good.

I didn't return his grin, for I didn't find a damn thing amusing. He already knew I'd been at the torso violation scene or he wouldn't be contacting me now. What role did he play in it? Why did he think I was working a case already?

When I still didn't respond, his smile sagged a bit around the edges and he sighed.

"I see. I know you saw Benjamin Satou yesterday."

"You know, a break-up is a separation, Trey. You shouldn't stalk your ex. There are regulations against that sort of thing. It's unbecoming of a T.A. agent, too."

Now, it had come together. Sure, Daniel had run a coordinate search on Satou's wauto. I also knew that Daniel didn't tell me everything. He seemed way too certain that I knew more than I'd shared. Why else call me down to the violation scene? He could've given me that info over the telemonitor.

No, Daniel had wanted to see my expression when I saw the torso because he had *other* information. Probably fed to him by Trey. Damn Territory Alliance. The T.A. acted as an Inter-Territory regulation force. Each territory submitted their own candidates to go between them as a solid enforcement unit.

"I wasn't stalking you. I'm working." Trey zoomed in so only his face could be seen.

"That's what you call it? You told the regs he'd come to me. What bullshit did you tell them?" There was a very good reason why Trey had been labeled an *ex*-boyfriend.

"Okay, Cyb. I dropped your name to the regs. I thought you and that Regulator Tom were friends. The D.C. Regulators are out of their depths with Satou. It's beyond them. Hell, it's beyond *you*."

Beyond me? That's saying something.

"I warned you about using my name in vain. If it's beyond me, then don't include me."

"You're not serious? We've done it before."

"We've done a lot of things we won't be doing again, Trey."

"Oh, come on, Cyb."

"That's the difference between me and you. When you tell a lie, you try to justify it."

He rolled his eyes. Leaning forward into the telemonitor's screen, he sighed. "I don't want to argue with you. I wanted them to leave you alone." He rubbed his forehead as if already exhausted. His eyes closed and crept open again.

"What are you doing in the District?" I swallowed my annoyance.

"I'm supposed to take JPEGs for that boyfriend from the moon colonies whose girlfriend is still here in the city. She's boinking everything that moves, including a couple of robots. Seems to have a fetish for the tattoo as well." Trey shook his head, but a grin remained.

Hatchlings were marked by the double helix tattoo at the base of their necks. Some, like Daniel, covered theirs up, but others, like Trey, wore theirs with pride. Hate groups and bias abound at the non-birthed people. The pendulum swung the other way, too—some people liked them to the point of making them a fetish.

"Any tattoo or just yours?" I hated that the question sounded jealous. Maybe I was.

He spread his wide hands outward. "Don't people trust each other anymore?"

"I know you're not talking about trust."

Knowing that the issue of trust was how our relationship ended, Trey stared at me for a long minute thinking. His gaze never wavered from the telemonitor. Anguish rested behind those eyes.

It could've been my wishful thinking.

"I could come over. We could talk," he said at last.

"We could, but we're not."

His eyebrows arched, his stormy gray eyes flashed in fury before disappearing behind his sunglasses. His face darkened with anger and an ugly sneer appeared.

"Yeah," he replied at last, but it wasn't kind. "I know. Shit still stings."

My own irritation rolled to the front of my face, burning as if ready to explode. He'd called and poked all my emotional soft spots, but I wouldn't let him know it. Not anymore.

"Tell me about Satou." I changed the subject to something safe, well, safer.

"Can't, but especially not over the telemonitor. Forget about it. The military's and the District's politics are all over that one. We're not together, but that doesn't mean I want you dead."

"Ditto."

He actually cracked a smile. "Good to know."

Trey didn't bring me any closer to discovering whether or not the real Satou had been in my office, but he had confirmed my suspicions. The District's army had their tentacles in Satou.

"I'd be a fool to think you'd listen to me and *not* go digging around. So, watch your ass."

"I don't have to because I know you will," I teased.

Trey shook his head and signed off.

Why had I entertained Trey's big brother routine when it had been so obviously misogynistic? Because it felt good to be wanted.

Speaking of being wanted, no sooner had I set the wauto in its designated spot outside my crumbling apartment building, the Fates continued their assault.

Once I cleared the pilot's side door, the smell greeted me long before his physical being appeared.

Wham!

A toxic mash of sweat, cologne, and grease rushed me. I pushed up on my elbows and spat. Should've seen it coming. How could I not? An ass-whooping at five in the morning?

My lips burned and something wet trickled down my chin.

Blood.

Wonderful.

"Stop pursuing Satou!" a male voice scolded.

I pushed back onto my heels and swung, mouth stinging with cuts from my own teeth. The vibrations from my fist connecting with the attacker's shin made my elbow ache, but I wasn't giving up.

The attacker collapsed to the pavement.

But he didn't stay there.

He pounced, his tawny fingers reached out toward my throat. I bucked, kicking as hard as I could at whatever body part was available. Cursing and hollering told me I'd made contact, and I scrambled up to my feet. The air swooshed out of my lungs and I bounced on my feet, fists pumped.

"Back off!" I shouted.

The attacker, holding his side, lumbered to his feet, but he'd lost some of his enthusiasm. Thick black hair hung down into his eyes, but his girth scared me. Bulging folds of flap threatened to tip him over. His eyebrows remained crouched over his beady round eyes. Nostrils flared. He threw his hands into a soft defensive pose.

"You serious? You want to try me?" A smile snaked across his face. "The great Cybil Lewis. Yeah, come at me, baby."

Who *was* this guy?

Why did he think I was great?

My mouth remained shut as he kept going, yapping so much his proverbial hole grew wider and deeper. Until he did something about his impulse control, we were going to have trouble.

"Who sent you?" I interjected.

Silence. The thug threw a punch.

I dodged it with a swift sidestep to the left. Ducking his left hook, I bounced around, throwing my own upper cut. Too busy talking, the thug grunted as my fist connected.

"Nice one."

I nodded in his direction. "Thanks."

He came at me, a combination of throws. A whirlwind of fists, some landed, while others missed by hairs. Slower than me, but stronger than an ox, the thug missed as we continued our uneasy dance. Each one he landed made me feel as if I'd been pounded with a sledgehammer.

One well-planted right punch sent me sprawling to the ground again. Skidding to a stop near my wauto's trunk, I decided this damn thing had to end.

Enough.

I snatched my pug out of its holster, and as the walking mountain came upon me, I shoved the barrel into his chest.

"Stop!" My body sung in wretched agony. "Who. The. Hell. Sent you?"

The thug froze. Confusion filtered across his thick features and his breathing escaped in short wheezes.

"I ain't telling you."

"You got until three." I welcomed the cold calm that came before I shot my weapon. "One. Two."

I opened my mouth to call the last and fatal number when thugster said, "I'll tell you!"

"Good. Talk."

The pug remained in the folds of his chest.

He smirked.

"I will shoot this into your flabby ass, and no one will be able to help you. Not from the District's compound. Hell, not even from down the fucking street. So start blabbering."

Double chins trembled.

"No fair! An even fight would be man to man, not with a piece. You're a cheater. Take away your weapon and you're just another bitch with her panties jacked up her ass!"

Whack! The butt of my pug connected with his face—all on its own. Honest.

The thugster spat and gave me a bloody grin as if he liked it.

Oh. One of those.

Great.

The pug's handle had a thin layer of scarlet where it cut into his face. He could have more pistol whipping. I'd had a real crappy morning.

"Last chance." I wrapped my free hand around his inky black shirt, twisting the material. This time I shoved the pug beneath his double chins. "You keep screwing with me like I haven't sent a bunch of people to death and the cradle."

Vinegar level at dangerous levels.

My tone caught him and he met my eyes. Whatever he saw there made him swallow, setting his jowls to wobble.

Or it could've been the pinch of the pug's barrel under his primary chin.

"I dunno. I got hired," the thug stammered.

"One. Two..."

"Pao hired me!"

"Why?"

"They gonna kill me."

"I'm going to kill you."

"They told me to send a message."

"Should I shoot the messenger?"

The thug's eyes suddenly exploded into saucer-size and he grunted.

"What's the matter?" I let go of his shirt and backed up.

My fingers connected to something sticky and wet just as I let go. I jumped back as realization dawned. The blossoming crimson spread like a wildfire in a dry forest across the thug's shirt. He grunted at me again and reached out to me, coughing up blood as he tried to grab me until he slumped forward. He became still.

Amazingly quiet, the early morning didn't produce any whines of lasergun fire. I dove closer to my wauto and waited, my pug in my fist. Blood had sprayed all over my shirt.

Where had the shot come from? Behind me?

Meanwhile my attacker lay sprawled a few feet from me, face down against the concrete. Unmoving, the thug didn't have any visible weapons on him, which caught me as odd. He couldn't seriously think a fair fight could occur out here on the street?

Perhaps he had been a messenger after all. If the army meant to kill me, they'd sent someone more skilled than this. Nevertheless, he didn't deserve to die. I had the feeling he wouldn't have killed me, only rough me up a bit to pound in the warning.

What has my world become when getting roughed up isn't considered bad?

Grimacing against the thick evening heat, I crawled around the wauto, searching the area for a glimmer of metal against the reflective lights and spots of illumination.

There weren't any.

I scanned the apartment building and the other thicket of bushes and homes for any sign of a sniper. I couldn't pinpoint any movement.

So who *had* killed the messenger? Pao? Who the hell was that? I had run into a lot of bad guys—and girls—in the District, but that name didn't trigger any memories.

Swearing at the fact I had to contact the regs, I stood up and unlocked my wauto. I kept watching the area outside while I unearthed my tablet from inside my vehicle. Once I switched it on, the power icon flickered. Great. Low battery. Instead of throwing it as far as I could, I shoved it back into my satchel.

Using the wauto's telemonitor, I contacted Daniel.

Daniel Tom. Regulator 3501. Unavailable. Leave your message now.

"Just got shot at by a sniper, and I've got one dead would-be assassin." I had almost decided to invite him to pay for my medical bill when the roar of an aerocycle snared my attention. No one in my building could afford such an expensive vehicle. I pressed END, and sighed.

Following my hunch, I got out. My instincts tingled. I'm an inspector, trained to look for patterns, but none of this added up. Still, I hurried back to the spot where the thugster met his end. Only scarlet splats and pools of lost life remained.

The body had vanished.

It had been less than twenty feet from my vehicle. I'd only turned my back for a minute.

Damn.

CHAPTER 4

ROUGHLY FORTY-FIVE MINUTES LATER, I stood beneath my apartment building's awning, with sweat dripping down my face and adrenaline making my stomach churn.

"What happened to your face?" Daniel's ragged facial features spoke of a long shift without sleep. He shoved a cigarette in his mouth and peered at me.

"Don't change the subject." I swatted his outstretched hand away from my chin. "You do like to make it hard for me." He smirked.

"You wish."

"Every night, Lewis," he crooned and leaned in close to my face.

I sat there, stony and silent. Pissed.

"You can't get all pissy. You hauled me out here. I'm off duty." Daniel coughed and then exhaled smoke.

"It doesn't look like it."

All around the landing lot outside my apartment, vioTechs processed and performed the duty of collecting evidence of my battle with the thug. Several times I caught them looking at me and shaking their heads.

"I got you to thank for that." Daniel rubbed his face and then stuck his cigarette back into his mouth.

"Yeah, well, you're welcome. They took my damn clothes, so what are they mad about? We can count this as partial payment for all the times I've come out on cases for you."

He only sniggered. "Like hell."

"There was a body here. I watched him die." I gestured to the container floating on one of the carts.

"Yeah, but what aren't you telling me?"

"Regulator Tom, you better see this." One of the vioTechs waved him over.

Daniel scowled as he stomped from my wauto over to her. I followed. She held up the scanner, and in big, bright green letters, the name Benjamin Satou appeared, blinking. A JPEG appeared in the upper right corner of the screen as well. The picture matched the guy who attacked me, but the name didn't.

"Well, I couldn't have killed him since he's dead." I folded my arms. "I saw the guy who attacked me. It wasn't Satou. You regs need better equipment."

Daniel shot me a dark look before turning it on the tech. "I already got a partial body with this DNA match."

The vioTech shook her braids in concern. "The scanners do not lie. That blood's DNA belongs to Benjamin Satou."

"Impossible." Daniel swore.

If you eliminate the impossible, whatever remains, however improbable, must be the truth, said a famous detective and a famous Vulcan.

And I needed to find it.

"Am I free to go?" I stood up.

Daniel looked up from his tablet. "Always to the point, Cyb."

"Well, can I go?"

"Yeah, what the hell. I've got your statement. You're pursuing violation charges against Benjamin Satou?"

"Against the man who attacked me, but it would be foolish. He's dead."

"Yeah, we don't even have a violation, so go ahead." Daniel waved me off.

"My face is evidence." At the mention of my face, my jaw began to ache.

"Go. You look like you got the shit kicked outta you."

Not wanting to test an irritable Daniel, I headed up to my bed.

———

It was a little after two in the afternoon. I reached the fourth floor of my apartment building with groans eking out of my mouth like water. After I released a deep breath, I got two thin, clear patches from the cabinet above the stove. My aching knuckles had swelled. When I reached to hold the box, my stiff fingers flashed in hot pain. I used my good hand to apply the patches. With a few toe stretches, I tried to relax my bunched up and strained muscles from my adrenaline rush. The patches used nanos to deliver pain reducers to the site of injury. After my battle in the parking lot with the porkster, I had more than a couple of injury spots. Still standing in the kitchen, I pulled out an ice cold bottle of Peck beer, twisted off the top, and started to drink down big thirsty gulps.

Who the hell was the porkster anyway? Benjamin Satou's name kept popping up on the DNA scanners. Why? Suddenly everyone had Satou's DNA? Hyperbole, but none of it made any real sense at all. And who killed the guy outside? He wouldn't have talked, but he had a real thread of fear in his tone and words. The man had proclaimed they'd kill him, and someone had done just that.

"Let it go, Cyb, let it go." I tried to turn off my questioning mind. If the District's army had meant to hurt me, they would've done it quickly and quietly. Not outside in a residential sector of the territory.

As I took another drink of beer, my lip throbbed. The anti-inflammatory kept the swelling of my lip at bay. Everything hurt, but the patches downgraded it to a dull ache in the spots I'd applied them. I walked over to the sofa and eased down into the cushions. I wanted to watch someone kicking the crap out of all evil-doers. Bruce Lee had been on yesterday. Maybe some old wrestling vids would be online today. Feeling my own adrenaline bubble burst, I toed off my shoes and clicked on the telemonitor. For the next hour, my body decompressed the ridiculous onslaught of information and attempted to do what Daniel had interrupted hours earlier my rest.

"That concludes our program," announced the automated programming. The telemonitor fell dark, turning itself off as programmed.

I convinced myself to use what little energy remained to shower off the rest of thug's blood and the fight. The shower's cold stream felt like ice pellets against my bruised flesh. Soon it melted into warmth, but it still stung. I leaned against the tile, watching the water turn to a pastel pink as the porkster's blood circled the drain, much like his life. My knuckles had begun to scab over. Bits of flesh, dried blood, and residue from the pain patches dissolved under the soap. My muscles throbbed, but the water felt good. Done, I grabbed my favorite towel, dried myself with soft pats and sat on the edge of my bed. I relaxed and closed my eyes to relish the quiet.

Until the telemonitor dinged and up popped Jane's face.

I closed my eyes and tried to ignore it. The last thing I wanted was another emergency, but the insistent alarm continued, so I finally answered.

"Go ahead, Jane."

She didn't smile. "Where are you?"

I quirked an eyebrow.

"Oh shit, your face. Long story?"

"Yeah."

"You want me to come over?" Jane stood up.

"No. I'll be asleep in half an hour."

She laughed. "Old people problems."

I shot her a glare that forced her to stop chuckling.

"So, tell me." Jane gave me her "I-mean-business" face.

"Daniel called."

"So, what did Daniel want?"

"Needed my insights on a case he's working," I replied. "A torso washed up in a cardboard box down at West Potomac."

Jane crossed her arms and looked at me. Her green eyes wide with wonder. "A torso. That's freaky."

So I filled her in on the rest of what happened and that Daniel would contact me once he found out more.

"What's freakier is he came back as Benjamin Satou."

"Bullshit," Jane snorted.

I nodded. "I'm going to dig a little deeper. Why don't you go by Satou's place? His address is in the files. Year 2140."

"What else I got to do?" With that, she signed off.

That was my line. I think we'd spent too much time together.

My body had staged an effective coup and took over all decision making, my brain be damned. The body wanted rest. My mind wanted answers. My injuries, exhaustion, and worn out muscles forced my brain to comply. Or else take leave of my faculties. That wouldn't be good, so I slept all night.

Who says I can't follow orders?

CHAPTER 5

THE INTRUDER'S breath smelled like garbage rotting in the noonday sun. It was hot on my neck and the sharp pangs from his knee digging into my back didn't improve my mood. Waking up to a real life nightmare put me into an even darker mood. There had only been one sound of footfalls, not more than one. He acted alone. More could be hiding outside, or in the apartment, but I doubted it. The warm trickle of blood down into my mouth irritated my lips, and it stung like the dickens. I relished the thought that my punch sliced open his cheek and he too bled.

"Leave Pao alone," he warned against my ear.

"Have you considered seeing a dentist?" I grunted back. With my face planted against my bed, it came out muffled. It didn't take Pao long to get a replacement for the thugster. How many killers did he have on his currency card?

"Dead bitches ain't funny." He applied more pressure, and I felt like my vertebrae would snap in two.

"But I am." The pain increased. I fought back the blackness that threatened to overtake me, but the nausea swelled up from the pit of my stomach. It wouldn't be held back for much longer. Just then I heard a click and the whine of a lasergun.

"Get up with your hands high, where I can see them, or you're going to be whistling Dixie through the hole I put through your chest."

Jane. She always had a way with words, and she also had her own passcode to my apartment for occasions such as this.

"Good thing I came by to check on you." The smugness permeated her words as she switched on the light.

"Yeah. Remind me to make you cookies." I grimaced as the pressure eased up and finally disappear from my back.

The intruder stood. Now free of his weight, I rolled over, sat up, and got a good look at him. He smirked at the situation he found himself in, as if he should have known better.

Jane's lasergun, a 357, pointed directly into the small of his back, forced him to obey her command. Sunglasses hid his eyes, and a black hat covered his hair. The same height as Jane, he probably weighed about fifty pounds more. But still, she was the one with the gun, so he held his hands up where we could see them. As I stood up, I felt my back ache and throb with pain. My knuckles were swollen from punching his hardened frame. And they hadn't healed up from the earlier fight.

"Name?" Jane barked with a little shove in the back from her gun.

The intruder said nothing. I balled up my fist, and with a hard right knocked his sunglasses to the floor where I stepped on them. "Again."

Jane shrugged. "Name?"

His lip bled along with his cut cheek. His dark eyes seemed to burn with anger, but there was nothing he could do about his situation. Had he stalked me a little more, he would have known I had a partner.

He licked his injured lip. "Don't matter who I am."

"Tell me about Pao. Who is he? Why does he want me dead?" I asked.

Jane provided the encouragement with another shove to his back with her gun.

He rolled his eyes, but didn't answer. Using an uppercut, I

punched him in the stomach, forcing him to collapse to his knees. My hand seared with pain.

"Don't make me ask you again," I growled, despite the horrible jolts of pulsating pain in my hand.

Jane snatched the hat from his head, nabbed a fistful of his dark red hair and forced him to his feet. He spat a bloody wad of something away from us. It landed next to window. I saw Jane frown in disgust. He was in danger of being shot simply for being nasty. He took in a deep breath of air, grimaced in pain as Jane tugged harder on his hair.

"Talk." I fought the urge to rub my hand.

"We ain't got all night. One call to the regs for violation of property." Jane pushed her gun's barrel up to his cheek.

Nothing like a pistol-whipping to motivate someone to talk, and this guy had used up all of my honey; only vinegar remained.

His eyes grew wide at the sight of Jane's weapon caressing his temple. The silent threat was effective.

"Please-please don't hurt me anymore," he begged, as his injured lip trembled. "I-I'll tell you what you want to know."

"We're listening." I wiped my nose on my sleeve. A long, smeared track of blood stained my sleeve from my wrist to my elbow.

He sighed. "Pao's going to kill me."

"Whatcha think we gonna do?" Jane grinned.

His eyes quickly scanned the bedroom. His hands also trembled and his forehead grew damp with sweat. His teeth tugged on his split lip, and when he spoke, his voice shook.

"I..." The intruder's face paled, and his Adam's apple bobbed like a bird had become stuck there.

"Go on," Jane said from behind him.

"Jane, something's wrong. Let 'em go!" I moved away from him.

Taking my lead, Jane backed away.

A look of complete discomfort distorted his facial features, and he gripped his stomach. He slumped forward and then fell face first into the floor. I rolled him onto his back and noticed the growing, dark red bloodstain that soaked up the bottom front of his shirt.

"What the...?" Jane squatted down beside me.

I reached down and lifted his shirt. Muscle, tissue, and blood lay scattered around a fist-sized hole in the intruder's chest. No cybernetic parts meant he had been human.

"Self-destruct?" Jane quirked an eyebrow as our eyes met across the body.

"I doubt it." I recalled the pained and confused expression on his face seconds before he met his end. "Good news though, he's not a Satou replicant."

Buried in the wound, something shiny caught my attention. "Hang on."

I picked up a tiny piece of material a little way from his stomach's exit wound. I held up a pink, blood-soaked transmitter. It was no bigger than my fingernail. "See? A homing signal. There's no telling how long the person on the other end of this listened. He most likely ate it without realizing it. These things are often disguised as candy or some other treat."

I smashed it with my swollen fist, praying the listener got an earful of static.

"Pao?" Jane asked, as she holstered her gun.

I nodded. "Again."

Adrenaline coursed through my veins and made my movements jerky. The intruder's presence had scared me, but I shook the sleepiness off and got down to business. Fighting for my life. Unfortunately, he was stronger than he looked. He took my kicks and punches without flinching, and shook the pain off like a seasoned professional.

"How's your nose?" Jane asked, knocking me out of the memory.

"Not broken, for once." I touched it to make sure.

"Lucky I came over when I did, he coulda killed you."

"Nah, I had it covered." I shrugged.

She glanced over to me and we both started laughing.

"You wanna call the regs…"

"Yeah."

I didn't want to contact them, but I had little choice. I did have a dead body in my bedroom. That would require a tad bit of explaining. Good thing I knew a guy would could get blood and tissue out of carpet.

Nearly thirty minutes passed before the wailing of sirens announced the arrival of the District's finest regulation enforcers. I underestimated how long it would take. I usually gave them too much credit. Jane sat on the sofa with her legs crossed, fingering her dreadlocks. My living room consisted of a bright orange sofa, a rustic wooden rocker, and a glass coffee table made from two cinderblocks and a slab of glass. Two floor-to-ceiling lamps occupied the left and right side of the corner walls. Some people had those wall enhancements that switched to different locales. Not me. When home, I didn't want to be anywhere else.

Please don't let it be Daniel.

I met the two uniformed regs at the door.

"You Cybil?" one of the regs asked as he walked in. His name badge identified him as Regulator Stevens. The fitted uniform threatened to rip around his belly and buttocks. I wondered when the District would re-instate its fitness requirements.

"Yeah." I swept my hand toward the bedroom. "He's in there."

Identical buzz cuts and suspicious eyes followed me as I led them to the bedroom. Once we reached the entranceway, they glanced at each other as if they couldn't believe a woman was taller than they were, but I figured they must get this all the time.

Regulator Stevens asked, "Can you tell us what happened?"

He held a handheld computer, a later model than mine, and it was smoky gray. One fat hand held a pen poised to scribble all notes down. Strange, I would think he would be carrying a recorder. He might have been; the personal computer might have been there to throw me off. Sneaky but not smart, these two regulators summed up the entire force.

"Sure," I said, bored by them already.

"What about you?" Stevens called to Jane.

"What?" she answered shortly without looking up from her hair. Her fingers had several locks in her palm, and she appeared to be checking them for something, probably blood.

"Were you here?" Stevens' mouth twitched.

"Yeah."

"Can you give a statement?" Stevens cleared his throat. "Miss..."

"Boxter. I'll give a statement." At last, Jane looked over to them. "Whatever."

Just behind Regulator Stevens, the other one remained quiet, but I caught him watching the exchange between Jane and Stevens with intense focus.

Does his partner talk? He was probably the one carrying the recorder, no need to speak. The partner's facial expression remained solemn. He didn't smile, growl or menace; he simply watched us from under his brow with dark, almost black eyes, like plum pits.

I ushered them into the bedroom and pointed toward the intruder. "So, I awoke from my sleep with this man threatening my life. He attacked me and would've killed me."

"He didn't have permission to be here?" Stevens didn't look up from his tablet.

"No."

"Is this gonna take long? We have work to do. You know, inspector work. And we have more of it to do, so...." Jane shouted from the living room.

Stevens nodded as if he understood, but I'm sure Jane lost him on the "inspector work" part. The partner remained solemn and silent. I left the door opened as vioTechs arrived.

I stepped out in the hallway to meet them. The sooner this mess was resolved, the sooner I could get rest and perhaps get this case solved.

"Body's that way." Jane jerked her thumb toward my bedroom with a smirk twitching at the corners of her mouth.

Regulator Stevens stepped out of the bedroom. He glared at Jane before turning to me. "Can we sit down somewhere and talk? I need a full statement of events."

His eyes moved swiftly from me to Jane and back again, as if he were trying to catch us sending silent messages. She stuck her tongue out at him.

I choked back a giggle. "My partner doesn't like regs. We can talk in the kitchen."

Stevens turned to his partner, then back to me. "I see."

We sat at the table and I recounted the early morning nightmare. I sat with my back to the sink so I could see into the living room. The other regulator sat with Jane. She spoke, too, and he appeared to be writing down her statement. The vioTechs walked in and out of my bedroom. I don't know how long I talked, but I said as little as possible. I didn't know how many Pao had on this currency card, so the less the regulators knew, the better.

Regulator Stevens stood and he tugged on the uniform in places it had crawled into. I looked away. Jane finished and came over to join us in the kitchen. The other regulator didn't look comfortable, so he probably asked her to come over. Jane had that effect on people.

"So, neither of you know why this guy just came in here?" he asked. His partner just continued to stare ahead, probably inventorying the kitchen cabinet's items.

"No," Jane and I said in unison.

His eyes narrowed. He didn't know what to think and the partner didn't really help him. So he said, "We may be back for more questions later. Don't leave town."

Jane snorted as they lumbered out of my apartment. The vioTechs had cleared out as well. They'd set up a bright yellow caution beam across my bedroom door. I guess they meant to come back too.

I said to Jane. "Are you scared?"

"Of them two? Hell no." She stretched and started laughing so hard tears really did spill over and run down her face. When she finished, she said, "I'm bushed. Where you gonna stay?"

"Right here." I patted the sofa.

"What about the door? Didn't he hack in?"

"Yeah, but who would be foolish enough to break in again, in the same night?" As soon as the words left my lips, I swore. I knew better than to tempt the Fates.

CHAPTER 6

BRIGHT, scarlet numbers gave the time as 1:13 AM and judging by the darkness, I'd slept about three blissful hours. Now awake, the questions remained and my body still ached. The distant roar of a maelstrom almost drowned out the heavy-booted steps.

The door rang.

"What now?" I pushed back the covers and slipped from the sofa. The rain clouded up my window, and night split. Lightening lit up the room in a flash before falling again to dark. My hand curled around my lasergun 350, and I pulled it out from the coffee table.

Nude but armed, I went to the door.

"Oh for fuck's sake," I groaned, seconds before my door slid open. "Stop. Right. There." My voice, husky with sleep residue, sounded more menacing than the lasergun itself. I was impressed. The whine of the lasergun punctuated my command.

With my free hand, I switched on the foyer light.

Trey smirked. "God, I love that suit."

I dropped my gun and swore. "I thought I changed your access code."

The six-foot-tall hatchling reached for me, and I shoved the gun to his chest. "Don't."

His liquid crystal gaze softened as he dropped his arm and the lust slid from his face. "Come on, Cyb. I heard you were attacked. That you killed a guy in this apartment. I had to come."

"My white knight." I lowered the gun and walked over to the sofa. Part of me wanted to hold on to the gun, just to have something to do with my hands. Every time I saw Trey, the itch to grab him, touch him, and grope him made me feel powerless. But, I couldn't get dressed and hold the weapon, so I put it on the coffee table and snatched on my robe. When I turned around to face him, my face felt hot.

"Damn it. I know you don't need saving..."

"Savior doesn't suit you," I said, voice an icy dagger, slicing through the air and his assumption. It fell in tone—deeper, more dangerous. "Kind of like trust. That doesn't suit you either."

"Trust? Are we back to that? Again?" He threw his hands up.

"Yeah. Trust. You broke into my apartment! What were you going to do? Cuddle in beside me? That's not creepy. And a complete disregard for my fucking boundaries." There was a sizzling anger in my words. "I could've shot you."

He stiffened. "No, I was going to crash on the couch until you got up. I wanted to be here in case someone else tried to hurt you."

"I can take care of myself."

"A well-thrown left hook can only go so far in a knife or lasergun fight."

"We all have to carry our packs, Trey, and I've been hoisting mine for years."

"Listen, what if it's not some random act of misogyny? What if I'm here, right now, because I love you?" Trey crossed his arms over his chest.

"Trey, do you hear yourself?"

"I know! I know it's stupid. I know it's presumptuous, and I didn't think it all the way through. I'm asking you to forgive the gaps in my apology. You don't know who you're dealing with. I heard on the 'Net, you'd been attacked, and I was in the Quad, so I came."

"What? Did you miss the T.A.'s class on tact and personal space?" I put my hands on my hips to keep from punching him. It didn't make me feel any better.

"You could've died today!" He closed the distance between us.

"I could die every day. I *am* a private inspector. If you hadn't fed my name to the regs, I probably wouldn't be in this damn mess anyway," I retorted, but the words lost their sharpness, blunted by the warmth of his gray eyes and the need to feel connected. Too often in this job, my humanity is dulled by the sheer violence of my day to day. It erodes my own humanity and lessens my enthusiasm to be around people.

Yet, there are times, like now, when I craved it, needed it, and I didn't even know I did.

But Trey did.

It had been nearly a year since my relationship with Trey had collapsed like a house of cards. My skin, the body's largest organ, was starved for affection; even with the pain skimming the edge of exploding, I wanted to be touched. Like all parts of the body, my flesh craved nutrients and fluids to sustain life, but it also required contact from another human. Human touch replenished passion and desire, faith and healing. Without that sensation of flesh on flesh, the body would continue functioning, but I wouldn't be alive.

Celibacy hadn't agreed with me. Contrary to popular belief, I don't hop into the bed with whomever wills it. I'm selective and cautious with my choices for coupling, but I won't lie to you either and say that I must be engaged in a committed relationship for sex. This wasn't the 19th century.

I have used my celibacy to my advantage. It has helped me stayed focused on other things.

For example, my apartment was really clean—before the dead body.

"You have a history," I whispered, all too aware of how wanting I sounded.

"We all do. Some of us are trying to overcome it." He smiled and when he did, his dimples appeared.

My knees threatened to buckle, but I wouldn't, no, *couldn't* go down that easily. I stood at 5'11", tall for a woman, and I came to Trey's chin, just under really. I fit well in his arms, and for the most part, enjoyed being in them. Even now, with the storm's roaring and the drumming of rain against the windows, I melted inside.

Trey saw it, because he reached for me once more, and pulled me into his embrace. "Come here, baby."

This time I didn't pull away.

In the distance, sirens wailed. Just another night in the District. Beside me, Trey lay sprawled out on the floor, completely counter to his structured and reserved awake self. His well-defined chest rose and fell almost in time with the clock's ticking. It's an ancient thing my grandmother gave me.

Yet, the clock didn't keep me awake. Questions did. Well, questions without answers. My instincts told me to keep digging into Pao and the multiple Satous. I tied my hair back, fought back the urge for a beer, and basked in the endorphin afterglow. Trey had always been a very good lover, but no matter what it soured in the end. This time, it would be on me.

Because besides being a good lover, he was also a very good agent.

An agent with information.

"Trey..." I nudged him with my good hand.

"Huh?" he rolled over to escape me.

"I need information."

I shook him, gently, and then more firmly until he opened his eyes.

"What's up? You okay?" He rose up on his elbows and searched the room.

"Who is Pao?" I readjusted the sheet tucked under my arms and covering my breasts.

Trey rubbed his face and laid back down. He folded his arms behind his head. "Pao?"

"One of the men who attacked me said Pao sent him. Just before he died."

"Did he give you any more than that?"

"No. A sniper cut our conversation short."

"A sniper."

"Military."

"I know that, Trey. You're holding back. Tell me." I punched him on the shoulder.

"Ow!" He laughed as he came for me, scooping me up into a bear hug and tugging me down beside him. His arms pinned me to the spot beside, and he rolled his 6' over me.

Snared in covers and man, I lay still. He bent down and lightly kissed my lips. When I opened my eyes, I found him staring at me. Even in the dark, I could feel his eyes on my face.

I waited.

"Pao is an extremely dangerous man. Background is he's some kind of business man with a lot of currency. So much that he's able to buy regulators, governors, and well, whatever he wants. The T.A. has been investigating him for violations in the Southeast Territories. He's been in the District for months now, and we've been watching, gathering intel, and investigating."

"Why hire someone to kill me?" I couldn't care less about his underworld dealings, but my life, that mattered.

Trey shrugged and his body weight lifted off of me and onto the air mattress beside me. His arm snaked around my waist and he pulled me closer to him. Sweat and sex lingered on his skin, and the new growth along his chin prickled my forehead.

"I don't know, but I'm gonna find out."

"Sure?"

"Sure."

"I know you're holding back."

"Hush. Come on. Go to sleep. Your body needs to heal," he said, his voice already thick with sleep. He planted a light kiss on the bridge of my nose.

Trey wasn't the only investigator with skills. He also didn't deny that he withheld information.

Well, wisdom is all in the execution, and I damn sure wasn't going to wait around on him to find out why Pao wanted me dead.

CHAPTER 7

RESTED, I woke early with only one driving mission—get answers. I wanted to break Satou and crack him open until all the hidden treats spilled out. I don't like being lied to. I expect it, yes, but I don't like it.

I also woke up and the other side of the air mattress lacked warmth. Sometime in the wee hours of the morning, Trey had shown himself out as quietly as he'd shown himself in. As my coffee brewed, I went to the door and deleted his security code—again. I could still taste his kisses on my tongue and smell his scent along my skin. New soreness in different muscles marked my every step. Now that my weary soul had been rejuvenated, I had work to do.

First, I had to go workout. I'd neglected it before and the thugster almost took me out. I decided to fly over to Padre's Gym even though my body hurt. I needed to clean out my lungs and slip in a much-needed workout. Plus, it would help my muscles to work out the kinks and soreness from yesterday's beating. Exercising would free me of the stress balled up at the base of my neck and pounding through my temples.

Exercise was about strength training and endurance. In this business, I often found myself up against bad guys who didn't think twice about punching, slicing, or stabbing a woman, as the thug who attacked me proved. I considered my workouts defense training. Occasionally, I could outlast and outmaneuver a bad guy (or very naughty girl). I slapped on a few more pain patches.

So, I headed down the stairs to the wauto. Thankfully they hadn't towed in yesterday, but I had expected it to be vandalized. Nope. Strangers probably thought it had already been vandalized by its faded and chipping paint, dings, and battered appearance.

Padre's took up most of the block between 51st and Summer. I sat my wauto down next to the sidewalk. As I heaved myself out of the pilot's seat, I scanned the area around me. Goosebumps sprouted across my arms. This was the same spot where I'd been attacked three years prior.

Now that I think about it, an intense workout with weights might be good too. Somewhere unknown violators hid in the District, hunting humans, and committing viler acts of human nature. Probably paid by Pao.

Normally in the summer, I jogged through one of the parks beside my apartment perspiring and suffocating from the stifling heat. Recently, I've become spoiled by Padre's, a sleek arena devoted to the chore of exercise. Padre's membership fees ranked among the ludicrous, but its high blast air-conditioned workout rooms and the automated equipment made the membership more than worth it. I didn't miss the harsh sun on my arms or its powerful rays frying the thin skin on my nose. Jogging through the National Mall did get boring, just running the same path over and over. At Padre's, the treadmills came with virtual reality goggles. My favorite running program was Mt. Fuji in Japan. The program was so detailed, so real, that I could see my breath in smoky wisps as I exhaled during simulation.

A few months ago, my favorite activity had been swimming, but there were too many people lodged into the pool, becoming a meat locker, to actually do good laps.

When I had put on comfy clothes—a pair of yoga pants and a well-worn tee-shirt that read, "You've come to a battle of wits, unprepared," I felt better, more relaxed. My weapon and its holster were shoved under the seat of my wauto—where it wouldn't do any good if I was attacked. Feeling a bit naked without it, I took solace in the belief that I could defend myself with my hands. Not that yesterday proved it. The pug decided the battle as the thug had so eloquently pointed out.

But I was alive.

Once inside, excitement seeped into my body, sending the beginning shivers of anticipation through me. Crisscrossing through the gym, I found an open treadmill and climbed aboard. Slipping the wireless music player into my ear, I scanned the channels on the treadmills console until I found one that was playing Mozart.

Perfect.

The treadmill commenced its running speed of two miles an hour through spiky hills and deep valleys. Closing my eyes, I let go as the speed increased, decreased, and mimicked mountain trails. When the pain crept in, I lowered the speed. I ran, thinking about nothing, letting all stress be pounded away by my feet. Not even breathing hard, I opened my eyes long enough to check my pulse and the time. Not even twenty minutes, good. I increased the speed on the treadmill, overriding the computerized system. The pain reminded me that I wasn't dead.

Who was the person in the box? Where was the real Benjamin Satou? The original came to my office. The bigger question was why? Why would the thug and the torso both have Satou's DNA? It didn't make any sense.

I grunted and tried to shake the questions whirling in my mind.

Like glue, they clung on.

No matter how fast I ran, they stayed right with me.

⊏⊐

Two hours later with my thighs smarting, my lungs heaving, and my arms throbbing, I headed for my parked wauto with a potent protein drink in my hand and a smile on my lips. Pain patches scattered over my body kept much of my agony at bay. Too weary to even change clothes, I carried my other clothes in my satchel, strapped across my torso. Humming and trying to ignore my fatigued body, I set about going to the office. Only just after one in the afternoon, I had downed two aspirins in an effort to relieve my stiffening muscles. Might overkill the pain patches with the aspirins, but hey, I wanted to feel good. In my soy milk induced heaven, I didn't hear the steps, but the deep cough I couldn't miss. It was beside me—too close to be comfortable or kind.

Swallowing and slowing a bit, I swiftly slammed my elbow into the person sneaking up beside me. I hurriedly spun toward the snoop, dropping my drink as I did so, and making the impact of my elbow hurt more with the force of my body behind it.

Daniel grunted, holding his stomach, and glowered at me. "Good to see you, too."

"You should know better than to sneak up on me. You owe me a protein drink!"

"You owe me a pain patch," he countered.

"What do you want?" I asked, hands on my hips, trying not to sound winded, which is what happens when I don't go to the gym regularly enough.

"Who says I want something?" He quirked an eyebrow. "I could be checking to make sure you're all right."

"Everybody always wants something. Nothing for free in this life."

He gave me one of those looks that said he was thinking something he wouldn't let come out of his mouth for fear I'd punch him. The remnants of my shake conjured more disappointment. Instead he smiled—a naughty mischief-lined grin.

"You know, Daniel. I've got work. So fuck off." I started for my wauto.

"Aye! Wait a minute. Got an update on our Christmas gift." His hands patted his pockets, for his cigarettes, no doubt. "Can you slow down? You're making me tired watching you."

"You tracked me down to tell me something you could've sent by text?" My heartbeat had slowed from its furious gallop. "Bullshit. Keep movin'."

"I know. Can you please slow down? Walk with me," Daniel shouted, before shuffling to catch up.

"We *are* walking."

"I mean at my pack-a-day pace."

As I slowed my speed to turtle time, I asked him again. This time with a controlled, clear voice. "Why did you come here?"

I didn't believe he had only come to discuss the box. No, Daniel wanted something else. My heart sped up its thump-one, thump-two routine at the grin peeking out from beneath Daniel's moustache. He grabbed my arm to stop me. He glanced over to me, grin still firmly planted on his face. His eyes, though, seemed pained, and he opened his mouth to say something.

I waited, my breath caught in my chest. My emotions with Daniel needed reigning in, not unleashing. Since his frequent visits to my apartment to discuss his murder cases, I realized our friendship was changing. In what way remained to be seen.

He glanced around the street before turning back to me. A nervous grin hovered around his mouth, and his upper lip disappeared into his moustache, which desperately needed a trim. His light brown skin couldn't hide the reddish tint that warmed his cheeks.

"I have the M.E. report." He held up a p-drive.

"The report isn't everything, is it?" I hated the sound of disappoint in my voice.

"No," he said at last, voice laced with fatigue, eyes not meeting mine. "I wanted to tell you at the violation scene, well at both of them..."

"What did you need?" I asked, overstepping his attempts at an apology.

He leaned against my wauto, his back on the peeling paint. With a heavy sigh, he stared up into the sky. We stood like that in silence for a few minutes. Not that we weren't accustomed to silences growing up between us. Since the big case involving the Irvings, Daniel and I have been doing it a lot—sitting in silence, I mean. Sure, but this one weighed on me, and I fought like hell not to look bothered by it.

He smelled like cigarettes and coffee, which I'd dubbed *eau d' la regulator.*

"I'm sorry for calling you down there. Now, it seems I've put you in harm's way." Daniel broke the tension. "It's my fault you got all knotted up in this."

"No, it's not. My coordinates came up in the investigation, so it makes sense to contact me." I avoided his eyes, for they truly were windows to the soul. And Daniel's soul had been through so much, seen so much; I couldn't stand the anguish in them.

He shrugged. "Yeah, but I should've just let you go home instead of calling you down to the scene the other night."

"Is that it? You came here to apologize in person. Ease your conscious?" I wanted him to deny it, to tell me the real reason, but he retreated into his shell.

"That's why I came by. To give you the M.E. report."

"Thank you, sir!" I let it go. I couldn't force him to convey his feelings.

We both laughed as we never said those words when we were in the service. The laughter fell away and Daniel's face struggled to remain blank. Something brewed underneath. So strong, it drew me to him.

"Did the army take over your violation case yet?" I had to change the subject.

Daniel coughed. "Not yet, but they're looking to cut themselves into the picture. I heard Captain on the phone with someone today."

"Seems like you'll be getting a new partner, sponsored by the District's military. That's how they stay in the case, without outright taking over."

He shrugged.

"I wanted you to be my partner." It came out in a hoarse whisper. Light brown eyes met mine and the ache in them seemed to reach out to me.

"I'm not good at enforcing regulators..." We'd had this debate before. Working for the Regulators ranked along the lines of burning to death.

"Or following them." He held up his hand. "Save it to your hard drive. I know."

"I'm sort of your partner already. The way you calling me out to your damn violation scenes." I stretched and winced. The pain patches had begun to wane.

"I'll repay you, so stop that damn whining." He raised his eyebrows, begging me to argue with him.

"Shut the hell up." I delivered the line he wanted.

"Nuthin' doin', Lewis," Daniel said, voice surprisingly husky.

He took out a cigarette and lit it with ease of someone who had done it a million times. Pushing out a puff of smoke, he reached into his shirt pocket and took out the tiny p-drive. "Here's a copy of the report."

I took the p-drive, but I had no place to put it. Yoga pants and a tee-shirt didn't come with pockets. "Bedtime reading."

He smirked. "Sure. Your bed'll be unoccupied."

"You wish."

Daniel's eyebrows rose. "You have no idea what I wish for, Lewis."

He had a point. I didn't. "See you later."

I got into the wauto and locked the doors before I did something I might regret.

When I checked the rearview mirror, Daniel's blue shirt was retreating down the sidewalk, his cigarette's smoke floating behind like a hazy scarf. It took amazing restraint not to call him back and invite him over.

What the hell was the matter with me? Trey's scent still lingered on the sheets.

I put my forehead on the steering wheel and groaned. The resurgence of pain filtered from their impact sites across my torso and out into my limbs. The pain packets had definitely stopped working. I'd be lucky if I could get up to the elevator without too much agony.

With an intake of air, I sat up and started the flight sequence as I once again tried to bury the issue.

I couldn't love anyone if I was dead.

CHAPTER 8

WHEN I REACHED the office building Wednesday around eleven, I reaffirmed my commitment to solving this case. Not for payment, but for my own damn ravenous curiosity.

Landed, I got out of my wauto. Growing more annoyed, I tried to force myself to relax. Despite sleeping through the night, my body craved more sleep and pain nanos, in that order. My mind wanted answers. Where the hell was Benjamin Satou and why did the thug, the torso, and damn who-knew-who-else have his DNA?

First, I had to bring Jane up to speed. When I came through the lobby's doors, Jane remained where I'd left her the day before—at her desk.

"Didn't think it was possible for your face to look worse," Jane commented without looking up.

"Still better than yours," I retorted.

"Bout time you showed up." Jane shrugged as she went back to her computer and using almost the same forced tone she brought out for her adversaries. "You've got a visitor."

"Where?" I picked up the cup of coffee Jane had already made for me. She was getting good at the administrative office stuff. Maybe I wouldn't hire a new assistant. After Martha's death, we hadn't had a lot of applicants for the job.

"Your office."

"Who?"

"Satou." The first slip of irritation came through. She tried for indifference, but failed with miserable and obvious clumsiness.

"Satou?"

Jane nodded.

"The guy from the other day?"

"Yeah, but no. He ain't the guy from the other day. But he gave his name as Benjamin Satou. You know anything about this?"

"I'll explain it later." I softened my own ice-sharp tone. Hot java in hand, I headed to my office.

"You ain't got to explain to me. You the boss...I—the underling."

She shrugged and returned to her laptop. She scanned the keyboard for the right letter. I would've liked to have a few minutes to talk to Jane about her surveillance efforts, but nothing doing.

Benjamin Satou. No doubt hidden in the shadows of my private office had tried to break into my computer. That's what I would've done if left alone in a private office.

Sighing, I carted my cup of java and my attitude to my private office, where seated in the sole visitor's chair was a man. When he heard the door open, he turned around, but didn't bother to smile as I approached. He wore black shirt, pants, shoes, and probably black socks too. A somber streak of dullness. His hair had been closely cropped to his head. He looked lethal, lean, and lonely.

I set the coffee on my desk and booted up my own laptop. While it chugged on, I twisted around to face him. It became obvious why he didn't smile at me as I entered.

He hadn't noticed. Absorbed in something beside the door, he visually searched the wall of my office as if it had been built with golden currency cards.

"You're Benjamin Satou." I made it a statement.

Startled, he spun around from his place by my honor wall.

"Oh, hello, Miss Lewis. I can call you, Cybil, yes? Yes. What, uh, happened to you?" He stared at my face, and then his gaze moved up and then back to my face again.

"Hazard of the job." I didn't want him in my private space. But, if I wanted to resolve this case, I couldn't deny him entry.

Well, I could.

But that wouldn't get me what I wanted.

I put the coffee down and took my gun out of its holster. "You want to tell me why you're here?"

This dark-skinned, handsome young man didn't look a lick like Satou. These men weren't clones. Something else was going on. Some government level experiment. Something out of a science fiction movie. I knew that if I scanned him, this man's DNA would come back the same as the torso and the thug.

He turned to me, and his blue eyes struck me hard in the chest. Those eyes—those eyes wept over Charlotte Satou's disappearance more than a decade ago—right here. In this office.

Those were Benjamin Satou's eyes.

"I've been discharged by the army. You helped me before, so I thought you could work your magic again," he began, hands in his pockets.

A chill zipped up my spine. The déjà vu forced my stomach to knot. My heart's beat increased steadily. Strange. The being seemed to have Satou's memories, but he looked nothing like the haunted and war-ravaged cyborg. Except those eyes.

"Help you with what, exactly?" My fingers wrapped around my gun, so I almost felt better.

Almost.

He swallowed loudly, his Adam's apple bobbing. "Look, I know I betrayed you the first time. Char, Char had been set against me. You understand?"

The story sounded the same, but accent and diction differed from the Benjamin Satou I knew. Still, I couldn't escape his eyes. Heartfelt. Genuine. Whomever this man was, he *believed* he was Benjamin Satou.

"Where is Charlotte now?" I put the desk between us.

"Deceased."

Frank. Flat. Not as mournful.

"I'm sorry to hear that." Sounding every bit as if I wasn't sorry at all. "Who takes care of your cyborg parts now?"

He frowned, caught himself, and then forced a laugh. "Cyborg? There's no such thing! It's against the District's regulations to even attempt to augment a human body with robotic parts. Robots are servitude and manual labor."

My flabber was gasted, but I kept my face blank.

"Would you submit to a DNA scan before we go any further?" I walked to the door and called out to Jane. "Bring the scanner."

The lanky man pondered. "Why? You have something against hatchlings?"

"It's just a precaution," I explained.

"I'm not comfortable..."

Again the feeling that something about him was strange caused my stomach to tighten. Jane stood in the open door of a closet where she searched for our DNA scanner. We had one, but we didn't always use it.

He saw insistence on my face because he added, "Yes, of course."

His restless eyes traveled on to other things behind me. Nervous twitches, ticks, and unsettled gestures gave me pause. No robotic parts, my ass. Maybe he didn't know it, but I'd bet my last bit of Peck beer that he, probably like the others, had been a cyborg.

As he sat down, my gut rumbled in warning. I shook it off and waved Jane in. Who was he? None of these people had been Benjamin Satou, so who were they? They weren't clones. None of them looked alike or bore any resemblance, except this one's eyes. The District had regulations against that, too.

Soon we'd know more about *this* Benjamin Satou.

Jane snapped on her plastic gloves and glee stretched across her face. She held up the scanner, its needle capped. Seated in front of my desk, Benjamin Satou glanced at me and then back to her with a twitch of his lips. I'm sure he wanted to stalk right on out of there, but nothing doing. Jane barred his path.

"Hold that hand up." She looked across him to me. "You know how this works, right, solider?"

He scowled at her tone, but remained silent. She jerked his right hand up to the desk, splayed his fingers, and focused on his index finger. When she rolled the hand palm upward, he shrank back, but she held it firm. Without so much as a warning, she stabbed it with the needle. A single droplet of blood bubbled and balanced on its tip.

"Hold still." She cackled and wiped his fingers with a cotton ball.

They still called them that even though no cotton had actually been used to create them.

She took the swab stained with a scarlet smudge of blood and ran it across the scanner. Within moments, the beaming smile on her face melted.

Benjamin shifted in his seat. "What? What does it say?"

"Don't you know?" I interjected.

This Satou seemed unsettled by Jane's silence. He flopped back in the seat, crossed his legs and his arms, and frowned like a child denied a toy.

"Of course I know. She just acted like I had a disease," he huffed.

"Or cyborg parts." Jane lifted up the scanner with the results facing her.

Before I could deduce the results from her expression, the door to the lobby yawned open and in marched three men, all dressed in ebony—tee-shirts and slacks. Steel-toed shoes clunked heavy against the floor as the very solid, very muscular, uh, *gentlemen* halted at the new receptionist's desk. They'd better not break that. I just replaced it.

I guess I was going to have to fill that position at some point.

"What do you want?" I came from around the desk, out of my private office, and stepped out into the lobby.

A fierce-looking man stepped forward. "Lewis. Looks like you put on weight."

Anderson Sean.

Mercenary. Muscle for hire. Mean.

"Still sucker punching people?" I could do mean, too. A cold chill spilled down my spine.

Anderson Sean and the people he worked for had left me for dead behind a dumpster years ago. Daniel had rescued me. I glanced back at Satou who had thrown his hands up in frustration. Jane had already come out of the office, and she snapped her gloves off as she did so. Her face set to deadly pissed off.

Back when Anderson Sean attacked me, I didn't have her.

Now I did.

The odds have changed.

Considerably.

The others were military. They had that look.

"Why are you here?" I put my hand on my lasergun.

Anderson Sean shrugged his chunky shoulder. "Although you're always sticking that ass in places it shouldn't be, I'm not here for you."

Jane's eyes narrowed like he shouldn't be checking out my bottom.

I agreed.

"Someone already tried to make your face prettier," he added with a laugh.

I shrugged. "Yeah, but at least I'm still breathing."

Anderson smirked.

"I'm conducting an interview, so either make an appointment or just leave. Either way, get out." I reached for the lasergun.

No, I'd been wrong. Not military. The military moved in quiet engagements, not brash and overtly obvious intimidations. Despite what the movies portrayed, the District's army wouldn't be this clumsy or overhanded. This stank of Pao.

"Oh. Hello, Sean." Benjamin Satou greeted the men as he poked his head out of the private office. "I'll be five more minutes."

Anderson nodded. "We'll be outside."

Jane didn't move.

The trio marched through the doors and out into the hallway.

Benjamin frowned. "Sorry about that. Are we done?"

I spun to face him. "How do you know him?"

Satou shrugged. "Work."

"What work? The army just dropped you like a hot aerocycle engine." Jane came closer to him, to us. She'd switched on her interrogation mode. Former Marine, she could do torture.

Satou fidgeted. "I'm employed with a private security firm. Sean is my trainer."

"I wouldn't take too many notes." I leaned back against the desk. "What company?"

Satou shoved his hands into his pockets. "Mendel Security."

I nodded. "Why did you come here anyway? You're working. You seem, well, grieved."

Again he twitched—a whole body endeavor.

"You gonna seize?" Jane's eyebrows rose.

"No," Satou snapped. Then to me, he said, "I'm here to..."

He stopped and confusion spoiled the rest of his handsome face. "I dunno why I'm here."

I slowly stood up, my fingers itching.

He hesitated. With a wipe of his hands on his pants, he looked at me with those eyes—*the real Satou eyes*. Uneasy, he cast another nervous glance at Jane. She'd gone to her desk and had dropped the scanner on it. Ignoring it, she braided her dreadlocks into one thick plait. Her nimble fingers worked their way down the length of her hair with rapid and practiced speed.

I waited.

He seemed ready to speak, but unable to do so. The twitches at the corners of his mouth conveyed as much. Still, he stood rooted to the spot between my private office door and the lobby's exit. Puzzlement stained his face.

"Cybil, I woke up this morning with a burning desire to see you. I got in my wauto and came. Every waking moment today blared that I contact you. I can't explain it." He ran a hand across his buzzed head.

"So, you don't know why you're here." I watched his face fall.

"No."

"Jane, the scanner's results…"

"He's Benjamin Satou."

No surprise there. I expected those results, but across from me, the soldier relaxed with relief. When he caught me looking at him, he tucked it all behind his smile.

"See there. No surprises. I'm sorry for wasting your time." He nodded toward Jane.

She ignored him.

"Cybil." Again, he looked like he wanted to say more, but didn't.

As he left, he tossed me a wave, but panic—or perhaps confusion—lingered in the shadows on his face.

CHAPTER 9

"TELL ME THE REST OF IT." I turned to Jane the moment the doors hushed close.

Jane looked up. "It read his DNA as Benjamin Satou."

"But?"

"But there's something more about his scan. DNA determines how we look. If he had Satou's DNA, he should look like him. He doesn't. So either the District's database is fucked up, or some new, scientific fucked up research is goin' on. He don't look like him at all."

"None of them did."

I'd had the same thoughts, too. Could there be something in the epigenome that could be used to alter their appearance? My inspector-in-training had grown so much in the last few years. Her insights had been spot on. So, if the torso, the thug, and the youngster who just left my office all had Satou's DNA, why didn't they look like him?

"We need to dig a little deeper." I spoke more to myself than to Jane. "But, the Mendel Security company is owned by the Association of Genetically Engineered Humans."

Jane stood and picked up the scanner. "Yeah?"

We stood in quiet thought until Jane spoke, her green eyes

flashing. "Cyborgs. The AGEH. What did the torso's autopsy report say? Just like aerocycle parts, they should have identification numbers."

"Cyborgs aren't legal, so there isn't a tracking number. I did get a copy of the autopsy report." I recalled the p-drive Daniel had given to me.

"What'd it say?"

"Dunno. I—I didn't have time to read it."

Jane shook her head. "That would've been the first thing I did."

"Yeah well, you didn't get the crap beat out of you yesterday, did you? Or ambushed at the office?" I adjusted the pain patch on my hand and headed back into my office.

"Touchy! It's not the first time you'd gotten your ass kicked, so no big whoop."

I glared at her. She dissolved into laughter.

"Oh the fresh-faced optimism, I mean apathy, of youth." Once the door closed, I went to my laptop and put in the p-drive. Jane followed, still chuckling. She stood behind me as the file unfolded on the screen. I'm sure that Daniel would be fired on the spot if they knew he had sent over the report to a citizen.

Jane pointed to the screen. "There. Right damn there. Nanos had been discovered. Smudges of oil. Clamps that could've been from something mechanical."

I nodded. "The torso's limbs had to be cybernetic. Those were removed. The head cut off, but the limbs..."

"...weren't cut off, but removed, forcefully, but not laser sliced like we thought."

"The medical examiner obviously doesn't know about cybernetics, but the torso must've been cyborg, too. So, the army had begun replicating them—from Satou's DNA. The thug probably had cybernetics, too, but had been removed before the entire body could be sliced open by the medical examiner."

"The army or the AGEH." Jane leaned back against the window sill behind my desk and crossed her arms. "Why? Why leave these parts all over the place? Why did that other Satou come to you today?"

I shrugged. "I think *original* Benjamin came to me because he knew about the other replicated soldiers, but due to some internal programming couldn't tell me. The grief he felt over the use of his DNA, maybe even his parts, bothered him. He wanted me to investigate."

"And you have." Jane crossed her arms and shrugged. "He could've fuckin' asked. Like a normal person."

I shut down the computer and stood up.

"Oh, yes, but Jane. He isn't normal. Nothing about any of this has been."

She snorted.

"This has been one long chain reaction of grief."

We stood in quiet reflection for a few moments. The gravity of the situation sickened me, infuriated me. I glanced over to Jane. "What about the original Satou?"

"I sat on him yesterday. Went about his business. Grocer. Boxing. Back home."

I frowned. "Nothing suspicious."

"Nope. Boring for a cyborg." Jane pushed off the window sill.

"I'm going to head on over there. He and I need to talk." I picked up my satchel.

When I emerged from my private office with it on my shoulder, Jane stood by the lobby's doors.

"I'm drivin'."

———

Benjamin Satou opened the door with a weak smile and a strong odor of whiskey. He looked at Jane and then to me. With a nod, he stepped back and gestured for us to enter.

The small house looked more like a studio apartment, with its crowded living room and stunted kitchen. No room for a table, or much movement, the room held a tiny two-eye stove, a sliver of a dishwasher, and square cupboards. Used glasses and bowls lined the floor. Discarded wrappers, cloth napkins, and food takeaway boxes lay scattered amongst the living space. Someone needed a maid—or a mother.

It looked like a single man lived there.

"I figured you'd come around sooner or later." Benjamin plopped down onto the worn sofa in the living room. He sat close to the edge of the cushion, his arms loose around his knees. With eyes like Christmas lights, he searched my face. "What happened to you?"

"*You* happened to me. Would you believe someone whose DNA scanned as yours tried to kill me?"

Satou blanched and looked uncomfortable. He fidgeted before shuffling farther back into the cushions.

"I—I don't know what you mean." He crossed his arms and tried to look calm, but his right leg bounced non-stop. Despite his body language, he seemed ready to talk. He sighed.

"You hear about the torso down at Potomac?" Jane asked.

"Nope. Don't watch the telly much." Satou seemed to be folding in on himself.

"Benjamin, I know you're not responsible for what's happened to these other men. I need to know who is behind this. Someone is replicating your DNA and using it to build cyborgs."

Satou reeled to his feet. "You've got to get out of here!"

Jane went for her knife. "Settle the fuck down!"

"Listen, all this drinking and hatred is being sent to the wrong address. You're not responsible. Tell me who is."

His face clouded over in anger. "You don't fucking get it! You can't outrun, outfight, or outgun these people. You just stop existing. A fucking file that's deleted. Gone."

"Who?" I asked, my honey level dropping faster than a Ford cargo craft. "Give me a name."

He swore, sweat pouring from his face. "I. Can't."

"Tell me what you can." I stood up, attempting to reclaim some civility.

"The man who came to see you. His real name had been Jonah. He'd been recruited for the Cwall program."

"Cwall. Cybernetic Weaponry for ALL."

"How many were in the group? How many kids?" I didn't think the District's armed services would allow any of their test subjects to escape. Sloppy play if they did.

"Most were kids. They didn't live long enough to become adults."

Jane growled beside me. "How many made it?"

"Four, not counting me. Even though the war's over, those in charge of Cwall wanted to try it. To build superior soldiers. I was the prototype, but you know that already." Benjamin stood up. The sound of engines whirring broke our silence.

"It?" I wanted to hear him name what I had suspected.

He rubbed his eyes. "Cybernetics."

"The other four are cyborgs." I made it a statement.

He nodded, wincing as if to say it aloud physically hurt.

"Why didn't you tell us that at the office?" Jane interjected.

"I couldn't," he admitted. "The subroutines prevent..."

"But you can now?" Jane's eyebrow rose in question. "Bullshit."

"No. I mean, yeah, I can tell you now because they've canceled the program. Before, two days ago, my internal programming blocked those classified files."

Jane glanced back at the door and the windows. "We need to get out of here. The military isn't gonna let him tell everything without killing us—and him."

Satou didn't seem concerned. He reached for the glass beside him on the end table. The amber liquid sloshed as he snatched up. Without pause he downed it, winced at the bite of it, and then reached for the bottle again.

"Cyb. Let's go," Jane encouraged.

"Why did they end the program?" I had to know despite Jane's antsy behavior.

Satou closed his eyes and when he opened them again, the pupils seemed to swim in their sockets. His slack jaw and relaxed posture spoke to his intoxication. With a grunt, he rubbed his hands together.

"It failed. The nanos failed." He grinned. "My DNA is indeed unique."

"So they tried to mix the nanos with your DNA so the others could accept the implants, like you could. That's what failed."

Jane nodded. "That's why their DNA scanned at his, but I bet if the District dug a little deeper, they'd discover the nanos inside held Satou's DNA."

"Chimera," Satou coughed out.

"Chimera?" Jane scowled.

"Satou has chimera DNA. That type of genetic is composed of distinct cells. This can result in two different blood types or subtle variations in form. The army used Satou's DNA with nanos to attempt to get those men to accept the cybernetic parts. Genetics tells us it could've been transported via organ donation. With cybernetic parts snatched from one and given to another, those two individual tissue would have separate genomes. Instead, they began to change into *him*. The recipient's body would begin to reject it. I bet that's what happened to the torso."

"Or accept it. Then the person changes. Like the man who came to the office today. Cyb, you said he had Satou's eyes."

"Are we right, Satou?" I turned back to him.

"Cyb..." Jane's tone held the hint of warning.

Across from me, Satou's eyes became unfocused. The sweep of his hair had begun to light up.

"Who's Pao? Why does he want me dead?"

"Cyb!" Jane shouted, seconds before her blade landed squarely in the center of Satou's chest. "Duck!"

I dropped to floor, just in time to see Satou thrown backward by lasergun fire. The wall behind me caved in thunder. In the noise and debris, I scrambled to my feet and ran with Jane right beside me. We cleared the back door to the house amongst the crash as of the rest of the house crumbled.

We didn't stop until we reached the wauto, which we'd parked a block away. When I looked back in the direction of Satou's home, I saw smoke and the din of sirens.

Jane stood with her arms akimbo, her face grave. No doubt her pack a day smoking habit didn't support running for your life for a block and a half.

"The fuck just happened?" She tossed back her dreadlocks and panted.

"I think that's what they call tying up loose ends."

She swore. "I'm gonna need another blade."

I smiled. "Indeed."

CHAPTER 10

CLOSE BRUSHES with death did amazing things to stimulate the appetite, so Jane and I ended up at Big Mike's. Big Mike's downtown jazz club held all the charm of a restaurant, bar, and nightclub and occupied the spot formerly known as McCormick and Schmick's at the corner of 9th and F Streets. The remnants of the Spy Museum remained in burnt out and abandoned bygone glory. Big Mike's was known for his pasta as well as his jazz performances. Its cozy dark and moody décor shunned newer places' affinity for polished chrome and shiny metallics. No, this place felt lived in and loved. History hung from its walls like family portraits, outlining the restaurant's lineage. I sat at my favorite table, right in front of the stage, and waited for one of the servers to bring my pasta.

I had a Port in a Storm and Jane had a beer. We sat in silence, drinking and reflecting after placing our orders.

"He's told us enough." I broke the quiet.

"Yeah. That's why I'm worried. He's told us some shit that can't be proved." Jane leaned back in her chair, slouching down to get comfortable. She stared off toward the stage.

No, he hadn't. A lot of conjecture, but the story hadn't been new. The District's military, like other research and development divisions throughout the territories, wanted to gain an upper hand in the event of war. The carnage, the collateral damage left in the wake of that research left tossed aside like biohazard trash, didn't matter in the quest for the greater good.

"They tried to replicate him, their sole cyborg." I sighed.

"With modest success. When people gonna realize individuals are better? They should make one and then break the mold. Like God did with me." Jane shimmed in her seat.

I gave Jane a side-eyed glance and shook my head. Benjamin Satou had been unique. One of a kind. So successful they tried to replicate their success. How many times had that been performed in history? It was innate in us to mimic. It's how we reproduce, how we conform, and we survive. Making more of the one thing that's successful made sense, but these soldiers were people. That part of our nature allowed us to use tools, to practice agriculture, to grow beyond our limitations because, well, someone was successful at something and we copied.

We replicated those successes.

When I looked at Benjamin Satou and the others, I wondered if we couldn't have used our other human parts to acknowledge that these were people, *beings*, who were beautiful and talented as they had been born or hatched into the world.

"If only someone in the R&D division had appealed to his better angels." I took a sip of my drink.

Jane shrugged. "Angels weep while wickedness breeds."

"Is that Yeats?"

"Nope. Jane Boxter."

I nodded.

"What we gonna do?"

I shrugged. I'd been asking myself the same question. Part of me hoped by the time I got to the bottom of my glass, I'd have an answer. "We go find Pao. Ask some questions."

"You think that's smart?"

"Dunno."

"Safe?"

"Absolutely not," I said almost before she could finish asking. "You scared? You can sit this one out."

"Nope. You'd die if it wasn't for me." Jane signaled for another beer.

Across from us, the curtains parted, and on stage a woman with the body of a twelve-year-old started belting out tunes about God and grace like she'd lived for three hundred years. It seemed odd for such a big voice to come from such a slender frame. Still when she launched into Amazing Grace without musical accompaniment, my faith was replenished. I couldn't speak for the other patrons, but my soul was moved. She sang as if on stage at the Venus Amphitheater in front of two hundred thousand fans.

Behind the horseshoe bar Big Mike, his eyes closed tight, his massive bulk swayed in tune to the song. His muscle shirt revealed less muscle and flabbier bulges of flesh, but he had a strong heart —one of gold. I wondered if his rocking would interfere with his delicate balance on the barstool.

Wednesday saw Big Mike's role as restaurant play out a little less than on the weekend. Still all around people chowed down on pasta and tofu. People drank and laughed, listened, and languished in solitude. As the gospel tune flooded the rafters, I took out my handheld and surfed the Net for information on Project Cwall. Immersed in cyberspace, my case could have a solid base. I'd like to know more about the others.

One thing I discovered. Absolutely nothing—at all. No whispers by conspiracy theorists. Nothing at all. No scraps of rumor or hints of knowledge.

Swearing, I slapped it down.

Benjamin Satou haunted me. The damaged lives. Damaged goods. Aren't we all?

Deciding to switch off my heart's bleating, I picked up my handheld again, deliberately blocking all attempts of Satou thoughts to interrupt. My surfing kept me occupied. Somewhere in my notes was an itch that hummed for scratching. My handheld resembled a

PDA. I couldn't afford one of those, so I kept the handheld. It stored loads of information and performed a wide range of functions.

Before I could ask, the waiter dropped my pasta off at the table along with a thin handheld—the bill. I double checked the tally. I settled the tab with a few swipes of my thumb, which drafted out of my bank account with speed that bothered me.

It took a hell of a lot longer to earn the currency than it did for me to spend it. I've got to learn how to cook. Just because it's automatic and computerized didn't make it infallible. Just like robots. Some people trust them without fail.

I don't.

And no, I'm not paranoid about mechanical devices. The other day, I read an online article about a robotic taxi driver that kept a customer in rotation for four hours around the Washington Monument. The damn thing tried repeatedly to discharge the passenger by pressing the ejection buttons, but they were malfunctioning.

Saved the passenger's life.

Leaving the paid tab at the edge of the table, I turned my attention to my drink and meal. Jane started in on her vegan meal of something grayish in a brown sauce.

"So, you heard anything else about the torso? The other Satou?" Jane blew a smoke stream out of the corner of her mouth. Her first cigarette of the day.

"No." I sighed.

"Nothing from your favorite regulator?" Jane peered through the smoke at me.

"No, but there's no proof of the thug who attacked me, no body, no violation. Outside the M.E. report, Daniel's been quiet."

Jane sighed. "Sucks though. To know that you've been replicated. How many others are walking around with that funny-ass DNA?"

I looked at her through the haze. "It's scary, but for the real Satou, I think *living* terrified him. With the horrors of war blunting your emotions, when the quiet sits in, you have so much more to battle through. PTSD is a terrible and laborious thing."

Jane nodded. A former Marine, she understood the callous nature of war and the wounds it wrought. She continued smoking as I took out my stylus.

No one hired me, well not officially, and there hadn't been any payment. With the hush put out by the military, the silent violation of Benjamin Satou and the replication of his cybernetic parts and DNA didn't sit well with me. Maybe they didn't see him as a person, being a cyborg, his existence didn't even register as anything in the District. His humanity had been stripped into nothing. Then they killed him.

Instead of speaking my outrage, I wrote, my pen hardly stopping to ponder before I exhausted my knowledge. Like rain, my brainstorm released a brief but furious squall. Leaving it alone for a bit, I munched on the pasta.

Wednesday might prove to be a rather productive day after all.

Jane nodded at the stage. "I like being an individual. There ain't no body like us."

"So kids are out for you, huh?" I hide my grin behind glass.

Jane shook her head. "Even if I had 'em, they're still individuals."

"Touché, and that's not exactly a no."

"Not that you would be having a kid anytime soon," Jane tossed back. "You can't count your niece either."

"Pass." I waved her off. When Jane waxed philosophical, I knew I was in for a long lecture.

"How about after dinner we head over to the corporate office of Mendel Security?"

Jane nodded. "What else you gonna do tonight?"

I laughed, but stopped at the music ended. Across the restaurant, one of the telemonitors showed an avatar reporter and what remained of Satou's home in a live feed in the background.

"Hey, turn that up!" I rose from the table and drifted closer to the screen.

Big Mike nodded.

"Reports are the house on McMulligan had a gas leak and the

owner, Private Benjamin Satou had fallen asleep while smoking, causing the explosion..." The reporter's overly chipper voice failed to convey the seriousness of the scene. "Regulator officials maintain this was not a terrorist attack..."

"Those lying bastards..." Jane whispered under her breath.

We went back to the table.

"It's being covered up and who has the power to do that?" I forked in some wheat pasta, chewed, and chased it with a swig of my drink.

"Currency chic or the government."

I nodded. "Mendel Security."

"Tonight."

CHAPTER 11

THE QUESTION KEPT me preoccupied until we reached my wauto and I noticed the clarity of the sky. The night's velvety darkness was free of clouds, but I could still only see a few of the stars that sparkled from millions of miles away. Overhead, aerocycles, crafts, and wautos flew past in lighted lanes to their destinations. I climbed into the wauto, exhausted but unwilling to go home and do nothing. Jane got into the passenger side, quiet, focused, moody. Typical Jane. I felt restless, and despite my mental fatigue, energy continued to push my body onward.

We flew across town to the western sector of the District, toward the office of Mendel Security. I slowed down until I came across the one-level metallic building. It took up half of the block. How much security did they house here? At nine o'clock, the place appeared to be closed. The front parking lot was empty. I flew around the block and set down behind the place.

"Looks like no one's home." Jane checked her lasergun's barrel.

I didn't get out of the craft. Evening traffic, and several people brave enough to come outside to walk around, didn't make this the ideal time to search the place. I hated stakeouts, but if Jane was doing it, I could, too. I recalled the days of training to become an inspector with Robert Morgan and his PI company back in Denver.

As the low man on the totem pole, I got stuck doing thousands of hours' worth of stakeouts that I neither enjoyed nor openly complained about. With only three other women in an office of fifty men, I didn't want to be weak. So I did them, but I really, really hated it.

"We gonna just sit here?" Jane sighed, and slouched in the passenger seat.

"What have I taught you? We don't just go in guns on blast." I tsked and shook my head.

"Yeah. Yeah. I need a cigarette." Jane snorted and got out of the wauto.

The hours crept past. First, I took notes on what I learned from the people who tried to kill me. That took about an hour and thirty minutes. Jane walked around and smoked like a busted wauto exhaust pipe. Next, I read back over all the notes on this case. The electronic pages contained at least twenty pages' worth of notes, not counting the ones I had yet to add. Some of it still rolled around in my head, attempting to match up like floating puzzle pieces in the dark.

After an hour or two of toying with the notes and the possible subplots of this case, I put the handheld back into the satchel and groaned. My neck started to ache, and my back joined in to complain. My eyes burned from strain and the workout of reading page after blaring white page of small fonts. Jane said I had a large purplish bruise right in the spot where the intruder had planted his knee. I hadn't told her I already knew because Trey had pointed it out. Although stiff, my knuckles seemed less puffy and more normal. The pain patches helped with swelling.

"What exactly are we waitin' on?" Jane asked as she slipped into the passenger seat for the third time in two hours.

"Pao. Henchmen. When people want to do something they shouldn't, they usually do it at night."

No one came into or out of the warehouse at the rear of the building. Deserted, the place seemed like it had been forgotten, but I doubted it. Someone wanted it to look that way.

"Come on." I got out of the craft to stretch my legs. Sitting in a craft for hours didn't provide great circulation to the limbs. My dry throat itched and I wanted something to drink. "Let's go take a look."

"Yay!" Jane squealed.

It made me smile. I did love her enthusiasm.

I locked the wauto, leaving my satchel behind, but ensuring I had my non-regulations skeleton keycard. We crossed the street to the rear of the building, the section that looked more like a warehouse. The building sat in complete darkness. In the back, a barbed-wire fence protected the warehouse, but showed no signs of wear or prolonged exposure to the elements. New. Someone wanted the worn place protected. I took off my shirt and tossed it over the top of the fence. With a leap, I attacked the fence and with two steps, I was over, making sure to avoid the charged top. Jane followed.

She tugged down my shirt, and I yanked it on. Sure, it had holes and snares, but my body didn't. I considered it a win.

Just then, a pair of headlights flashed across the warehouse from the front. I crouched down and crept to the building's rear. The back door lacked scratches, rust or excessive wear. I could smell the moisture of approaching rain clouds. With a swipe of my unauthorized skeleton keycard, the doors opened.

The place smelled like a hospital and was pitch black. I felt around the wall to stay away from walking into something dreadful. I heard Jane's soft footsteps behind me. I could make out stacked boxes just inches from me once my eyes adjusted to the gloom.

"Move that crate," a male voice boomed through the night.

We crept forward and peered into the dark. A light flickered on at the other end of the warehouse. Two figures in white coats talked together. One appeared to be a woman with reddish hair; the other, a man who wore a hat with the AGEH emblazed in blue lettering. I couldn't make out much more, but getting closer would expose us. The few crates were stacked back against the rear warehouse doors only. The rest of the floor was empty. Coupled with the shadows, they hid us from view.

I could only listen to their voices echo. The woman carried a crate, the size of a small dog. She put it down onto a metal shelf. Behind them, three sets of double doors, spaced out at equal intervals, led to other parts of the warehouse.

"Come on. We've got work to do. General Pao said another one died, so we've got to clear this place out." The male's voice had been stained with irritation, and the woman didn't say much in return to his orders.

General Pao? You'd think Trey would've told me the man ranked in the District's army. All military. The businessman persona melded with the general one. Great. Just perfect. Not only did Pao have enough currency to buy the entire Midwest Territories, he also had access to military weapons, specialists, and funding.

The male scientist waited next to the central set of doors. Beside him, the woman dusted off her hands and swiped her key card through the doors' release. She then stepped up to the retinal scan. Within moments, the doors slid open and they disappeared inside.

I waited half a second, then quickly came out of hiding. Jane crept out behind me. We inched farther into the room. The humming of machinery and the soft whirl of the air conditioning gave the place an otherworldly feel. Adrenaline pumped through my veins and my heart raced with excitement. Jane had holstered her lasergun and removed her phone. I walked to the metal shelf and peered inside the crate.

"Jane." I waved her over.

Three trays, containing about twenty vials all labeled *Satou*, filled the crate. The empty vials only bore the label. Some held a dark red fluid, most likely blood. Satou's blood. Right here. Proof positive of Satou's claims that they'd taken his blood and thus, his DNA, to try to create more like him.

"He didn't lie." Jane took out her phone and snapped a picture of the vials.

"Set the recorder."

"Okay." She nodded and moved around the warehouse, recording.

Benjamin Satou's death would have meaning. I couldn't let them get away with snuffing out all these lives just because they could. None of this meant a smoking gun, but these vials meant they were doing something with Satou's blood. I slipped one of the vials into my jean pocket.

Those AGEH scientist said they intended to shut this place down. The central set of doors required retinal scans, so we couldn't get in. But the other two sets of doors needed only a keycard for entry. I contemplated an entry but had no idea how many others worked behind those doors.

"I've got everything in this area." Jane patted her phone. "Already uploading."

"Good. Let's go."

She nodded. It had been a long day for both of us. We left the warehouse through the back door.

Once back in the wauto, it occurred to me as I set the flight sequence that for a security company, Mendel Security hadn't been very secure. I thought about that for a minute. Would they leave it so vulnerable because it wouldn't be there for much longer? Satou had said the Cwall program had been closed down. I wanted another crack at that warehouse before all the dirt got swept under for good.

"Tomorrow, I'm going back to the warehouse."

Jane nodded, a slow grin on her face. "Me too."

"Well, by *me* I meant *us*."

"Course."

⸻

The next morning, I pulled on my black sweats, grabbed my hair, tied it into a ponytail and woke Jane, who'd slept on my sofa. As she dressed with hurried silence, I packed blanket, flashlight, and my pug. I walked into the kitchen to check Satou's blood vial. It remained in my refrigerator. Despite being dead, essences of him remained.

Jane, dressed in plaid boxer shorts, a black muscle tee-shirt and heavy, white cotton socks, held her coffee and an unlit cigarette in one hand. Her dreadlocks were parted and braided into two long plaits, one on each side of her head. She looked like a little girl, except for the cigarette. She inhaled her cigarette and squinted in its smoke when she exhaled. Her tee-shirt exposed her toned and athletic arms. She sat cross-legged on the white-painted, wooden kitchen chair.

"Fuckin' hate mornings," she croaked, still not quite awake.

In a few years, she'd have that sexy smoker's voice and lungs filled with phlegm.

"Bring your phone. We'll need to record items." I nodded at Jane's cell phone lying on the coffee table.

Jane grunted.

Once we reached the wauto, she had already lit the cigarette in her mouth. Damp morning air slipped into and lingered in my nostrils. We flew across empty, early morning lanes. We reached the warehouse in a little under twenty minutes. Nearly, six o'clock in the morning, Mendel Security still remained locked up tight, but a wauto sat parked out front. I couldn't tell if someone had gone in early or had parked it there and disappeared to somewhere else.

I didn't have time to work it out. The sooner we got in there before they removed the good, incriminating stuff, the better. We headed around to the back, to the warehouse entrance. Once again, Jane and I climbed over the security fence and into the warehouse area.

The crisp early morning air filled my chest, sending chills down my spine. It propelled me forward, and I heard my heart pound in rapid excitement as I approached the back door. My skeleton key card opened it with ease. Once inside, I quickly clicked on my flash-light. I flashed the light around and listened for sounds or voices. We made our way past the crates and down to the three sets of double doors. The room, icy and unheated, didn't seem so large.

I walked over to the doors closest to the west and listened. The thick metal doors hindered any sound. For all I knew, there could be a closet on the other side of the door.

I had to risk it. With a swipe of my skeleton keycard, the doors opened.

"It smells like a hospital in here," Jane whispered, her cell phone at eye level as she scanned the area.

The smell of antiseptics grew stronger, and I waited until the doors closed behind me before moving farther into the corridor. The entranceway definitely wasn't a closet. It led down a hallway. Several doors lined the hallway. The glass windows were frosted over for privacy, and the silence added to the mystique. The first set of doors we came to were locked and required a key card, retinal scan, and a hand print. The black lettering on the door read, "Nursery."

"I don't want to know." Jane walked on.

"Me either." I tried to peer into the window, but it was too frosted over. Giving up, I moved over to the door adjacent and across the hallway from the nursery. The unlocked door opened without the need for a key, and I found nothing but mops, brooms, and other cleaning stuff. This room really was a closet.

The room neighboring the closet did need a key card to open. Once I got in, the coldness made me shudder. That wasn't all that sent a chill down my spine. Once the fog cleared, I stifled a scream. Benjamin Satou, wrapped in plastic and tied with ropes, stared back at me with unseeing eyes and a look of sheer terror frozen on his face. Satou's last resting place didn't end in that bombing of his home, but here, hidden amongst the many vials, petri dishes, and liquid combinations of potions.

"I'm not sure what's worse. Death by fire or this." I turned away in disgust.

"Is that Satou?" Jane leaned closer. "Shit!"

"Yeah. Come on." I hurried out of the freezer and checked the other two doors in the corridor. The poorly lit area made each step a slow and careful one. I skipped one of the two remaining doors.

Locked with tighter security than my skeleton key could open, I left it alone and gave the last door my attention. This one opened with ease and contained several rows of different vials, each labeled with people's names. None I recognized. Jane kept recording as we moved along. Not necessarily a freezer, but definitely a refrigeration unit, the walls were lined with shelves. The top two shelves contained snake venom, and the third tier had various spider venoms.

We found more vials, but also some DNA specimens on the shelves on the fourth tier in petri dishes, closer to the ground. Along with the specimens, I discovered the embryos. Dish after dish of embryos was stacked six to twelve deep in sealed boxes along the first level of shelves. I wondered how long they had been there. Someone was definitely creating something using human embryos, but these could be legitimate hatchling work.

The final door, with the tight security, at the very end of the corridor read "Lab." I figured the door led to the same area as the central double doors the two white-coats from last night had disappeared into. No doubt they were doctors or technicians.

I checked my watch. It read seven-thirty.

"We should go." I tapped Jane on the shoulder.

"Right."

Sneaking out of the warehouse the way we'd come in, I felt sad. Satou didn't deserve this. He volunteered to serve his territory and deserved happiness, joy, and safety. He deserved not to be used like an old pair of run-down shoes being passed on from person to person.

The sun's bright rays barely peeked over the horizon, and yesterday's heavy cloud coverage receded under the glare. The mists evaporated as well from the sun's growing presence, and Jane and I made it back to the *wauto*.

"What're we going to do?" Jane asked.

"I dunno."

"You dunno?"

My honey supply was quickly running low. I may have to resort to using vinegar, and no one wanted me to use vinegar. The day had already been too long and I was quite ready to go home.

"No, I don't." It sounded much sharper than I intended.

"You're crabby."

"Yeah, and you're not helping." I crossed my arms.

"Cyb..." Jane started, but stopped.

"Jane, listen, you—" I began as I fumbled for words.

We got into the wauto, and the smooth and quiet flight to my apartment gave me time to be reflective about what we'd found and what to do next. Jane appeared lost in her own thoughts.

Just as well. I didn't have anything to add. Normally, I'd have something to say to brighten my inspector-in-training, but my own internal darkness eked out, blanketing everything.

Leaving only gloom in its wake.

Once I set the wauto down outside my apartment building, she got out without a word. Stalking toward her aerocycle, her shoulders hunched against the morning sun.

"I'm sorry, Jane," I said softly to her fleeing figure. I knew how hard apologies were for her. So her behavior seemed right on par with the Jane I knew. She'd be all right.

I didn't know if I would.

CHAPTER 12

SUNDAY ARRIVED with its usual speed. Three days had rippled by me. Too lazy to leave the apartment, I felt like the energy had been sucked out of me and deposited in a secret vault that I didn't have the key to. The last few days weighed on my shoulders, pressing their gnarled talons into my skin and stealing my strength.

One day—I can't remember which—the District's vioTech people came and removed the caution beam. That same day, I'd had the carpet in my room replaced. I wanted my space, but I wanted my peace back more. The waves caused by the case, the attacks, and Satou's haunting dead eyes crashed into me. They clawed on me, threatening to pull me into the abyss.

I sat in my bed, covers pooled at my waist, my favorite black tee-shirt on, sans bra. The coffee mug rested on the nightstand, but the jalapeno jelly and peanut butter sandwich remained in my right hand. As the text scrolled across my tablet's screen, I thought about General Pao. His actions couldn't go unreported. He damaged people's lives as if a virtual reality game. Pawns and puppets.

It didn't sit right with me.

The ding of my telemonitor cracked my quiet. Along my nightstand, beside my coffee, my handheld lit up too. Daniel Tom. Regulator.

"What's up?" I answered with a smile, but a tremble in my stomach.

He ruffled his hair and lit his cigarette. Peering intently, his eyes already looked tired. With a grunt, he answered. "I got a body down here. DNA scanner reads Benjamin Satou. That's the third one in a week, counting the torso."

"Another Satou." How many more? All those embryos in the deep freeze.

Daniel hunched closer to the screen. "The higher ups have closed it all down. Sent the vioTechs home. Labeled it a suicide and done. I wanted you to know."

"Suicide my ass, but thanks." I sipped my coffee and grimaced at the bitterness.

"I know that look. Just leave it alone."

"What do you mean, leave it alone?"

Daniel scratched his moustache and stared at the window. His shoulders sagged.

"It's over, Cyb." Daniel huffed.

"No, it isn't. He tried to kill me. He's murdered so many others. One of them there now."

"Allegedly."

Satou had to be telling the truth. I hoped he didn't die for a lie. "Just because he's a General doesn't absolve him of the responsibility..."

"Yeah, it does," Daniel insisted. The screen shifted and rolled with a smear of colors before adjusting to his face again. "Two attempts on your life and you still want to chase the big dog. Let. It. Go."

I crossed my arms. Did he know me? Why would he even ask if he did?

"You don't remember me finding you near death and tossed in a compost heap? No? Right. You were unconscious! I'm tired of watching you get hurt, Cybil. For what? You can't fight the governors. You can't fight these people."

"Someone has to." I ended the call.

Daniel wanted to protect me, but it had everything to do with me being female. If a man had been wanting to investigate General Pao, he wouldn't advise them to back off. Nope.

"Suicide my ass." I slammed my now empty mug on the nightstand.

Restless. Frustrated. I showered and dressed to head into the office. I gulped down another cup of coffee, draining the mug of its contents, and hurried from the apartment. Sunday or not, I needed to get some answers.

I'd just put coffee on to brew at the office when the lobby doors slid back.

"Hello. Is this the office of Inspector Cybil Lewis?" A tall, thin man smiled at me, but his lips twitched. With a buzzed cut and hawkish nose, he stopped just inside the doors and scanned the room.

"It's on the door." I put my hand on my pug. No one seeks a P.I. on a Sunday, unless they want trouble.

"Right." He didn't move.

"Who the hell are you?"

"And they say you're a good P.I." He peered across that beak of his nose at me.

From this distance, I could tell he stood as tall as me, with his shoulders squared and rigid. The man held all the hints of sharp edges shone by military toughness and rock-hard rigidness. A solider. Had General Pao sent yet another assassin to try to kill me?

I put Marsha's old desk between me and the stranger, my mind whirling. Stupid Cybil! I foolishly relaxed my guard, believing the attempts on my life would cease now that Cwall had ended.

"What do you want?" I wrapped my right hand around my lasergun's handle.

"You are an insistent pain in the ass." He coughed, and stepped farther into the lobby. The elegant, cream suit cost more currency than a year's rent on my apartment, judging by how the fabric flowed and refused to wrinkle. The bright orange tie had flecks of gold. Shiny black shoes caught the overhead lights. They looked glossy. Polished.

"Who the hell are you?" I took the gun out of its holster. No point pretending I wouldn't use it or threatening him with it. It made me feel better.

His smile widened, but it didn't fit his face. It looked like it had been attached. "I'm General Pao."

"General Pao?" Doubt made my words sharp. "Right. And I'm Abraham Lincoln."

"No, you're not Lincoln. You are Cybil Lewis, born Christmas day, 2117. I gift I wish I could give back."

"Hey, fuck you too, pal."

He continued as if I hadn't said anything. I'm certain General Pao only heard his own voice—and loved it.

"...But I do like your spirit. You've been sticking your nose into my business and you've been quite the nuisance. Tenacity I wished some of my employees possessed."

"Are you recruiting me?"

"No, but you're running around, trying to get information. I'm here to tell you." He stopped smiling.

Along with a lasergun blast to my heart, right?

Instead of that, I asked, "Why? You've tried to kill me!"

Oh, the arrogance beamed from him like those ancient picture of white Jesus. The sheer fucking privilege lodged in his posture, his demeanor, and his tone forced my grip to tighten.

"I did, but you proved hard to kill. So, I've taken another approach. You've also broken into my warehouse and forced me to get rid of my favorite prototype..."

"Benjamin Satou was a person, not a *toy*."

"Not by the time we finished with him."

"Get out! Get. The. Fuck. Out!" I lifted the gun and felt the usual cold filter down over me. All emotions leaked out and what remained, a numbness of absolution in what action I'd take.

"Put down the gun. Stop this foolishness. You can't win, Cybil."

"No?" I blew out a sigh.

"No." He looked me in the eyes.

"Watch me." I fired.

I wasn't thinking about consequences. My sole focus resided in seeing him suffer, watching him hurt for all the victims he'd injured with his callous approach to life and humanity.

The beam tore through his polished suit and into his flesh. He didn't flinch. No blood emptied from the wound. Nothing. General Pao smiled, stuck his finger into the torn fabric and flesh and wiggled it around.

My flabber was gasted. "The fuck?"

"As I said, you can't win. Perhaps you should sit down, Cybil Lewis."

Too shocked for words, I lowered my gun and sat down in one of the two visitors' chairs. "Cyborg?"

He shook his shiny dark head and adjusted his tie. My beam had singed the left section of it. "Robot. Full. Well, mostly. I still have a human brain, but most of me—well, over eighty-five percent —is not, as you would call, human."

"Why are you here?" I croaked. "To monologue?"

General Pao frowned. "To give you information, as I have already said. Years ago, when the territories were still somewhat united, the Defense Department came to me, and a group of other businessmen, about funding and developing cyborgs. The sci-fi movies inspired a number of the Defense Department's half-baked ideas, but this one was obtainable. Cyborg soldiers. I invested heavily in the research."

"But you closed the Cwall program. Why come here today?"

It all seemed to click home as the cold realization dawned. They didn't stop Cwall because it failed; they stopped it because something else worked *better*.

"Cwall is over. Satou is dead. All of the recruits are dead or living out their lives in citizen designations. In short, Cybil, this is an official cease and desist from the District's army to you, citizen. By regulations, I could kill you, but you've already proven you won't die easily. You'd give your life just to see me pay. You'd die happy knowing you'd won, and well, I can't have that."

For a robot, he saw with amazing clarity what many humans missed, until it was far too late.

"Your niece and your sister might not want to die for any cause." He spoke with a calm certainty that made my skin prickle. The hairs on the back of my neck didn't like it either.

"You have done your homework." I couldn't think of anything wittier or not cliché. My niece meant more to me than my life, and the fact that he knew it pissed me off. I lived daily with a bounty on my head. It's the penalty for the profession I work, but my niece didn't do anything, except be related to yours truly.

"I didn't get as far as I have by being careless." He came closer to me, chewing up the distance between us.

"You come to my office. Threaten my family. And you ask me to do something for you? You really are a heartless bastard." My hand clenched tight around the pug, and my honey level circling the drain. How many blasts would it take to put him down, for good?

"You broke into my warehouse, threatened my associates, and smeared my name," General Pao replied. "We are even. No?"

"No."

"We will part in agreement that we *disagree*. Do not come near me again. Some unfortunate things may happen to your family," General Pao reiterated. He ran a hand through his hair, yanked down his jacket, and left.

As soon as the doors hushed closed behind him, I slumped against Marsha's desk. I needed a drink stronger than coffee.

I pushed off the desk and went to the window. My office was located on the East Side of D.C. I could see the former United States Capitol from my office window on the sixth floor. The neighborhood wasn't the best, but it was cheap to rent space. The occasional homeless person or prostitute solicited for funds, but nothing dangerous happened here. In fact, the only violent deaths that had occurred in a six-block radius came from yours truly.

Me. Cybil Lewis. Private Inspector.

I'm nothing if not resilient.

It took Jane roughly twenty-five minutes to meet me outside the office. Her smoke swirled high into the sky. The gentle breeze brought tears to my eyes. The parking lot outside my office remained vacant. I wanted to go back upstairs and eat more cookies —anything to give me warmth. Something wholesome. Normal.

General Pao coming to my office didn't fit that definition.

But Jane wasn't done with her cigarette—or her questions.

"You just goin' to believe him?" she asked between puffs, her voice escalating. "I mean, he could be anyone."

"Yeah. But, I can't risk Nina." I crossed my arms against the crawling feeling over me.

"Listen to yourself! You're letting them get away with it." She threw her cigarette butt on the floor and mashed it with the toe of her boot. Her eyebrows knitted together in concentration. "You got a plan there, genius?"

"Of course," I said with a smile.

"Yeah. Let's do it." She shot me a quick grin.

"Let's."

EPILOGUE

SEVERAL DAYS LATER, Jane sat on the sofa of my apartment. A deep throb of stress slowly worked its way from the base of my neck up to my temples. It was time for my daily stress reliever.

"Malcolm said it would air tonight." I went into my kitchen.

I grabbed two cold beers from the fridge to chase the throb back to the base of my neck, if not out of my body entirely. I took three long drinks before returning to my living room. When I sat down on the sofa in front of the telemonitor, I took the remote and turned up the volume. Outside another storm rained down on the District.

"Thanks!" Jane took the beer and hugged my throw pillow to her.

The telemonitor had been muted through the advertisement.

"Cyb, now!" Jane sat up straight.

"Okay. Okay." I unmuted it and the volume balanced just at the news program launched.

The avatar reporter withdrew to a square in the upper right of the screen. The screen switched to a grainy video of the warehouse at the Mendel Security. The reporter continued, "Channel 18 News received this anonymous footage from the Mendel Security warehouse. This shows embryos, frozen, and vials of blood stored there. The owner of Mendel Security doesn't have a license for biomedical materials, but the Association of Genetic Engineers have denied all knowledge and claim the video is fake. The Territory Alliance continues to investigate..."

Jane looked over at me. "It's out there. The video we shot. You think Nina's going to be okay?"

"I didn't leak it. You didn't leak it. Someone hacked our files and pushed it out there to the 'Net. Channel 18 picked it up."

We'd done a lot to cover our tracks both virtual and physical. General Pao remained out there, making money, and making folks dead—all for currency.

"At least they're not replicating more soldiers." Jane shifted on the sofa, took the remote, and started channel surfing.

"No. Thankfully, I'm one of a kind." I glanced back out across the grayed sky. I'd started the ball rolling to get justice for Satou and the others.

"Yeah. Thank the heavens for that," Jane said.

The End

BONUS READ

Discover how Cybil met Jane, and how she first came in contact with Benjamin Satou in the short story, "Reunited."

REUNITED: A CYBIL LEWIS STORY

━━

reunited-[ˌrēyo͞oˈnīt' ed]- come together or cause to come together
again after a period of separation or disunity

ONE

THE SCARLET OVAL winked excessively as the crisp air bit into my cheeks. The cold, manufactured moon air left much to be desired. The oxygen mixture coated my tongue in a bitter film and I grunted, battling back the urge to spit. If I opened my mouth now, more than tainted saliva would spew forth—like curse words and more than a sliver of rage.

With teeth ground against each other, keeping all threats of violations at bay.

For now.

The laser gun's whine punctured the still tense air.

"Who are you?" the inhuman voice demanded. Gloved hands slung the cannon around narrow shoulders clothed in the moon colony's spacesuit style.

"Cybil Lewis," I replied, not even trying to hide my identity. With my laser gun and its holster hung up back in the D.C. Quadrant on Earth, I wouldn't be able to lie my way out of this one. No gun, so no threatening him into submission. Layers of nylon cotton blend kept me warm despite the frigid manufactured moon air, but the dread piling into my belly—it burned. The snitch's tip that Charlotte Satou was here had been suspect to begin with.

This ambush confirmed it.

I glared at the Southeast Territories Marine. The Southeast Territories' tentacles stretched into everything. So it didn't surprise me when I spotted the SE Marine badge stitched onto his shoulder. Yes, they would be in bed with the EuroRepublic's conglomerate of greed and nasal accents.

The tint on the visor shielded his face. Was it a robot? The moon colony wars had plowed on for over fifteen years now, so it wouldn't surprise me if they'd gone to using robots because the supply of humans had thinned out.

On second thought, no, the being behind the weapon breathed out and in, his ventilation mask unable to successfully strip that away. He carried the plasma cannon like he'd been born with it. But his stance bordered on sloppy.

"What are you doing here?" he asked.

"I can't tell you that. You want my telemonitor's IP address? That you can have," I said, giving him a grin I used to seduce potential clients. "As to anything else, well, you can't have it."

"I can take it," he leered.

"You can try."

With sternness riding through me, I stared at that visor, daring him to carry through the bluff.

Yeah, I was many things, but a blabbermouth wasn't one of them.

I didn't squeeze my eyes shut, but every muscle tensed for the oncoming plasma blast.

It didn't come.

I didn't *really* think it would.

"What are you doing here?" he repeated. With a hard thrust the barrel shot closer to my face. "Tell me! Now!"

"Threatening and yelling. Yeah, that'll get you what you want," I said, relishing the cool calm that washed over me. With coldness came resolve.

Stubbornness thou name is Cybil.

"You're an intruder." The ventilation mask stripped away all his humanity. "Whose side? The District's dogs? Or just a scavenger?"

I stayed quiet. Nothing I said right now was going to move the cannon blaster.

How the hell did I get here?

Two words.

Benjamin Satou.

A District Army Infantry man home on leave. He smelled like burnt oil and fidgeted like a robot on the blink of going permanently dark.

While staring down the SE Marine's wide barrel plasma cannon, I could see Private Satou as clear as that day several days ago...

Attempting to put his best face forward and to grab hold of the steeliness that soldiers must possess, Benjamin Satou looked me directly in the eye as he sat in my office. Oily, raven-black bangs didn't keep much of his despair from showing. Scars from flying debris or laser gun fire, and a long thick disfigurement etched along his left jaw spoke to the light touches of war and his involvement in it.

For him war wasn't pretty-literally.

"My wife is missing."

"How long?"

"Two weeks, give or take," he answered, short and to the point, the military conditioning taking over to shield and buffer whatever emotional turmoil whirled inside him. "I arrived home from the launcher at approximately 0700 hours. Upon entering my residence, I found it empty. My wife's belongings and clothing all appeared to be in order. The only thing missing is Char. Our wind automobile remained in its hanger."

The queer tick cropped up after each statement, like an old typewriter or blinking cursor for a software program.

"The wauto hadn't been flown? Last coordinates checked?" I asked, frowning a bit as the tick clicked again.

"I checked the autopilot's logs and the last coordinates visited but it was the grocery store."

"Any signs she'd simply left of her own free will?" I asked, my hand

gripping my gun tighter. Touchy question might snap one of his taut nerves.

That question received a scowl so severe I thought his face would fracture.

Jerky motion and unnatural turns, facial ticks that ran surprisingly in sync gave me pause initially, but he'd been referred by a friend.

"Continue," I said, wanting to keep the flow of information going now he'd decided to share.

"I, I thought Regulator Tom told you all this?" a sharp hint of frustration made his words tight.

"He told me some things," I replied coolly, fingering my laser gun 300's barrel. It rested happy and content against my thigh. "Other things I don't know. The point is I need to hear everything from you."

And he told me.

Now I wish he hadn't.

"Hands up," the soldier ordered.

"No," I said. "I'm not looking for a fight. I just got lost."

"Lost? You just wondered into the army EuroRepublic's barraks? During a war?"

"Yes," I said, the lie hardly making me breathe hard. "I got lost coming from that bar down the street."

"Yeah," the soldier snorted.

It could've been a laugh.

I took in a deep breath and kept my hands down.

I crept along the back pockets of the base to a designated rendezvous spot.

Instead of finding my contact, I walked into the gloved fist of said soldier.

"I said hands up," the solider barked, gesturing with the cannon blaster draped across narrow shoulders. "You going straight to the tanks."

"No way," I said, shaking my head. "I'm allergic to flotation gel."

"What?"

"Hell, no," I said with emphasis, and patted my left shoulder, remembered the 300 was tucked into its holster and locked inside my office safe. Damn. "Drop it. Listen, I'm looking for someone. Nothing more. Keep this up and we're going to have major issues. The kind that'll send you rotting in the pits."

Silence. Was he studying me? Checking out my figure?

Wham!

I stood up, my chest on fire where the soldier's boot had slammed into my chest. Scrambling around, I fought to focus. Someone had outed me. I doubted my contact waited, if the person existed at all. The problem with paid snitches is they're all violators of the District's regulations. So if they ripped you off, you couldn't report them.

I should've known better as the entire affair had become suspect.

Using the shadows I ducked and bobbed, the soldier's punches whisking by. I shot out a round-house kick and sent the assailant windmilling into one of the rooters parked nearby. The huge tires on the moon-buggy rocked it to its side from the impact. The glowing amber circle above the infirmary declared healing occurred there, but I wasn't seeking a physical remedy, only information. The clatter didn't seem to cause anyone to run out of the bubbledome-shaped infirmary.

He came at me again, clumsily slow, his stance askew. Probably dazed and winded by my roundhouse or drunk. It surprised me he'd even been able to stand after the solid hit. I need to get back to the gym.

"Argh! You fight like a woman!"

I waved him forward with my fist. "Shut up and bring it."

The soldier came at me, all arms and legs flying. *Who trains these guys?*

Pivoting sideways, I dodged the assailant. When he blew past, he turned and came at me again. Huffing like a worn out buggy, he charged me. This time I dipped to the left, his right punch coming much too slow. Without waiting, I threw a left and it plowed right into the guy's jaw. An *umph!* punctured the air.

He fell to the dust again, skidding to a stop against the rear wall of one of the barracks holding his jaw. Too much noise too often would cause someone to come and check.

The soldier shoved himself off the ground and inched into the light.

He lifted the visor and a face far too soft and feminine to be male came into view. As the helmet lifted thick cords of dreadlocked hair *whoosed* down to those shoulders far too thin to be male now that I gave it my full attention.

The perpetual dark floating along the edges of the night held many surprises. I considered myself officially surprised. Find Jane, I'd been told. Silly me. I figured that to be some cryptic code word. Using the dark sections the oval spotlights failed to illuminate, I disappeared into the shadows.

She removed the ventilation mask.

"All right, I guess you're safe enough to talk to."

"A woman," I whispered.

"I get that a lot up here," she said with a smirk.

She removed a cigarette from behind her ear. Soon, a crimson oval lit up the shadows of her face. Pillow plump lips curved around the cigarette and she smoked liked she'd been doing it for far too long.

"Sharp hearing," I said, recalling how she ambushed me.

She sucked the sliver of rolled tobacco before saying, "Heard you several blocks back." The husk of her voice skipping through the smoke rings.

Yeah, sure.

"Name's Jane," she coughed, sniffed, and extended her hand. She stepped closer, lowering her voice to a hoarse whisper.

"Cybil."

We shook.

"Moto's crazy, but she saved my bacon a bunch of times up here. She said you're good, so I owe her which means I pay you," Jane explained with a shrug. "The woman you lookin' for was here, two days ago. Maybe three. Days blend. Manufactured time screws up your biological clock and being off the planet does something funny to your mind and your body. Anyway, our twilight sweep picked her up with a bunch of other strays littering the outside crevices of the bubble bioms."

Beneath the bubble-shaped bioms grew plants, pools of water, and soldiers probably pitched tents and other outdoors activities. The moon's harsh, infertile surface wouldn't be able to create the resources needed without help from the bubbles. They're carefully crafted Earth in little handheld bubbles that expand until they were the size of stadiums.

"So, what else you wanna know?" Jane puffed out a nice series of smoke rings.

I liked her. She had personality and although her fighting technique needed some work, she'd been a trooper by agreeing to tell me what she knew. Moto's a crazy partying chick from the district's E801 Quadrant and she *did* owe me.

"Where'd she go from here?"

"Well she was processed and sent on to Martians knows where," Jane said and took a drag. A long stream of blue-white smoke sailed through the air.

"I don't get why she came here...to this base."

Jane shrugged. Green eyes squinted against the smoke. Her flawless ebony skin hadn't been eroded by time, but had been worn by cynicism.

A kindred spirit.

"We're in a war. People need aid, healin' and helpin', Cybil. She could've come for that. Bleedin' hearts rocket their narrow asses up here and try to bring some humanity to the humans all the time."

Sad. Those on Earth didn't realize the soldiers, generals, and doctors were all a bunch of people following orders.

"So, yeah she met up with that crowd," Jane said.

"Yeah," I said. "Right."

Our eyes met and we burst into giggles. She was too young to be this jaded.

"Look, thanks," I replied, shoving my hands into my pockets. "I've got to find her. I'll push on to the pits."

Jane shook her head. "Aye, words of wisdom."

"From a teenager?" I quipped. "I'm gonna pass."

Jane's face hardened, becoming stone serious.

"You got that look, the edge, like your feelins' been blunted by the dull daily blade of war. That's what my general calls it when he looks at me. So, turn on your freakin' instincts. There are so many dead dozens that we're using open cargo trucks as mass gravesites. The pits are crawlin' with body snatchers, raiders, and the freakin' hungry. Stay in the light. Though that alone won't save you."

I nodded. The pits housed bodies the warring military decided not to incinerate. Mostly civilians and the occasional defected soldiers. Moon craters had better purposes, but until the fighting ended, well, mass graves it was. Raiders looted the deceased for currency, jewelry, and weapons. The body snatchers came for experiments and black market transplant organs.

"I got it covered," I said, icing the words so she knew the lecture was wasted. "Been here before. Been doing this awhile."

"Uh huh," Jane replied, glancing toward the rumble of a crater crawler.

The vehicle sounded close. I needed to get gone.

Jane gave me a solemn nod and stepped off toward the rumbling roar's direction.

"Try not to die," she said.

TWO

THE GATHERING GLOOM infiltrated every nook of the EuroRepublic's moon base. For a decade several territories and the EuroRepublic battled it out for ownership of the extremely limited resources and land the moon offered. Regardless of how much blood was shed, no one won. Just clear losers all around.

I moved toward the pits with my heart heavy and my ears buzzing.

As I stepped along the gloomy infested back streets of the Euro-Republic's barracks, I thought about Benjamin's visit. Glittering fireworks set off in the north, and I for one was glad to be heading south. I passed gates and high-level security compounds in various bioms, but no personnel.

"Must be good to be on terra firm," I said to Benjamin as he sat in my office.

I tried to put him at ease. His muscles flinched and flayed on their own accord and he frequently hopped up from the chair and paced the length of my private office before deciding he should sit. Perhaps he missed being told what to do.

He'd only been back from the moon colony wars for a matter of weeks. Not near enough time to decompress or adapt to civilian life again. No doubt he awoke most nights drenched in sweat and screeching in despair. The echo of violence still rang loud and raw in his psyche. Who knew what those screams and cries and carvings spoke to him during the lush and lunatic landscape of dreams.

Darn it. Once a soldier always a soldier.

Through him I recalled my days with the DC infantry, I understood his horror and his hell with amazing clarity.

"You seeing the quad's shrinks and A.I. evals?" I asked, eyeing him hard, trying to pin him with my gaze, but he wouldn't meet it. His eyes jutted all over the place. My office décor didn't deserve so much attention.

"Uh, well, no, ma'am."

"You takin' the happy pills they give you for transitioning back to the planet?" I asked, not caring that my voice sounded harsh and unforgiving. He needed a rough verbal lashing, hell, he needed a punch in the face for failing to follow his commander's direct orders.

"No ma'am."

That wasn't good.

Benjamin Satou.

Solider. Husband. *Cyborg.*

A shudder raced through me at that last. I hated robots and the jury was still out on how I felt about people and robotic parts being combined. Theories abound about creating cyborgs, but to my knowledge there hadn't been any real progress on legislation or success on that front at least in the D.C. territory.

"I'm a cyborg," he explained with a casual wave of indifference, as if his hand could simply swipe away the mechanical ticking emitting from his person. "Sort of. I'm nearly 50% of robotics and nanos, and about 49% organic. Char is the doctor assigned to maintaining me." His eyes still glowed azure, but clear.

"How?" I stopped myself from launching onto my verbal soapbox regarding robotics.

"A few months after I arrived with my platoon to the front lines, I got blasted in an ambush. Whole chunks of me were blown off or damaged, according to the physicians. When I woke up, they'd fixed me with titanium based parts and other pieces."

Not liking it, but forcing confidence I didn't feel, I said, "Why waste the parts and technology on an infantry man? You're expendable. Why not input them into an elite squad of super cyborg soldiers? What you got that they didn't?"

He gave me a snarky grin.

"Doesn't matter. Your payment, please," I said, gritting my teeth to keep my curiosity at bay. "That's not counting expenses."

"Agreed." He extended hand higher, demanding via body language I shake it.

So I did.

Anything to get him out of my office quick.

"You don't like me," Satou had accused, but without whining. Just a statement of fact. "I'm a man, Ms. Lewis. Being a soldier is a job. Different than yours, yes, but beneath the vague label, I'm a human despite the parts."

That's debatable. One of which had the District's council deadlocked with creating regulations.

Instead I said, "To me, Private Satou, you're a client. The rest is immaterial."

No, but the lie expedited his exit from my office. The ball at the base of my neck pulsated with annoyance and sprouting stress.

"Regulator Tom said her last emailed message hailed from the moon. Any ideas why she'd email you there?"

Regulator Daniel Tom, an old army pal, had already given me the background on Benjamin's missing spouse, but some things you can't hear second hand. You had to get it straight from the source. In this business, you take referrals when you can get them. But that didn't mean I had to fall for anything—or anyone.

I saw what Daniel probably did when he looked at the young private. *Us.* Years ago, two scarred kids, emotions juiced on a steady diet of flight or fight exercises, and blood and bones and *death.* Our psyches had been ripped to strips held together by the thinnest of sanity.

Benjamin could've been me, Daniel, or scores of other war weary people punched about by violence. Yeah, Private Satou needed help. As a former soldier, I saw it because I went through it too. Luckily, when I came home from the line, I had Stephen to piece me back together.

Benjamin had no one.

"Dunno," he replied. "None of it makes sense. That's why I'm paying you."

He removed one of his gloves. With a quick lick of his thumb, Benjamin paid without prompting from me. His DNA matched his currency account and authorized it to transfer the funds from his file to mine.

"I'll get started soon."

"Thank you. Good luck finding my wife," he said, and stalked out.

Was that a threat or a confession?

I stared after him with my gut churning in anxious warning.

THREE

I SHOOK MY HEAD, throwing off the memory of Satou and the eeriness it conjured.

The automated day launcher gave the dark side of the moon some semblance of time, but Jane nailed it when she said it didn't flow here. Instead it lumbered and chugged along. How many days since Benjamin's visit? Even I couldn't be entirely sure and I wore my digital watch. According to that, I'd been on the moon's surface for about a day and a half. Outside the EuroRepublic's barracks and dome shaped camps, I avoided the spray of spotlights that illuminated the inkiness. Making my way to the pits and cargo stations, I thought about what I'd found out.

The burning question that continued to rotate around my head wouldn't cease.

What was Charlotte Satou doing on the moon after her husband had been scheduled to return to earth? Who was she anyway? Was she ever here at all?

It wouldn't surprise me to learn that Benjamin had murdered his wife and hired me merely to provide cover. He hadn't taken his treatment to return to a normal state since coming back on leave from the war. He continued to plow along daily in half-cocked battle mode. There's no telling what he'd done with her or *to* her.

With most of his body switched over to robotic automation, he might have had a short and accidentally done the dead. Hell, he might not even remember.

Nothing surprised me in this business anymore.

Not one thing.

That didn't feel right. Cyborg or not, Benjamin felt something resembling loss for Charlotte. His sentiment rang true, so it had to be something else gnawing at the edge of my consciousness. The smear of time and the manufactured gravity made me sluggish mentally and physically. I was missing something important.

But what?

A shadow glided out from the others and just as swiftly vanished.

Who the hell?

I spun around and searched the bleakness.

Had there been someone there?

I couldn't be sure.

A faint whirling swept through the air. I hastened my steps, not running, but moving with a purpose. I switched off my internal dialogue and focused on the bastard following me. Along this stretch of darkness, only the moonlight sphere attached to my jacket cast a long solitary illuminated line through the inky black.

I started again for the pits, but kept my senses on alert.

Footfalls fell silent as I kept walking. Still, the hairs on the back of my neck wiggled in warning. Someone followed behind me. And I couldn't catch him.

I slowed and tried to catch the person off guard. I increased my speed to lose him.

Both times I got nothing.

Still, the shadows swayed and played with my vision. Sluggish and tired, I couldn't be sure someone trailed behind me at all. Icy shudders shot down my back, aggravating the pit in my stomach.

Who would be following me on the moon?

No one knew I'd even come here, except Moto.

There, again!

The faint whirling reached my ears.

Someone *was* following me!

Fine. I took off running and dipped into the edge of blackness creeping along this pathway. I canceled my artificial light source and waited for the stalker to come running on by. Counting to a thousand, I waited.

My eyes adjusted to the growing dark, but not enough for me to see anyone.

I had banked on hearing them instead.

I waited.

No one came.

Either I lost them, or I had a serious case of moon madness.

You can guess which one I liked better.

FOUR

THE ODOR REACHED me long before the view became marred by bodies. Crumpled and broken, piled and plastered together in decaying mounds of flesh and fluids, the deceased spoke volumes in gasses, odor and mass. Flitting across these humongous mounds like flies at a garbage shoot, people dressed in one-piece suits and ventilation masks scavenged for anything worth selling.

The odor lodged in my throat and I kept coughing to expel it.

Nothing doing.

I reached into my satchel and removed a portal ventilation mask. It hooked over my ears and molded to my face, suctioning to the area around my mouth and nose. It filtered clean air through and took out CO_2 out, while at the same time stripping the air of all but pure oxygen. My mouth tasted like I'd been chewing on plastic, but better that than inhaling the air.

I walked by one of the hundreds of cargo crafts overflowing with the dead. Who were these people? Did their families know of their demise? Stumbling over a discarded boot, I cleared the strange oval of crafts and into what appeared to be a series of pits, some natural, others created. How best to find her?

Ask.

The navy-clad body snatcher rummaged through the corpses

like a person in the produce section of a grocer. He jumped as my voice reached his ears, so intent on plundering whatever he sought.

"Excuse me," I said, missing my gun as much as my apartment right then. "I'm looking for a woman."

The jumpsuit and hood sort of hid his gender, but I could tell from its tight fit, the person in front of me was a man. He turned visor-clad eyes to me and even with his mask on, I could see him frown.

Don't make this hard. I don't want to add your ass to the cargo craft's collection.

"Ain't everybody," he snorted in a dialect that rang of the Eurorepublic's conglomerate. "This one's mine so move on."

"Listen, I'm looking for someone who's fresh, alive," I added, pulling out my currency card. "She got dropped by the SE's twilight sweep a few days ago."

I detected the snarl through the mask's heavy ventilation and I pushed on, folding the card back into my pants pocket. My satchel lay strapped across my torso with it's opening in the front. No sooner had I cleared his cargo craft, did the impish body snatcher plow into his pile, forgetting I'd even came by.

Someone on this rock had to have seen her. I'd been clawing my way around the outer arc of the pit cluster for more than a few hours. And I hadn't been alone.

Snatchers and poachers, raiders and rebels and I had spent quality time shuffling through the muck. Surely someone who worked this hell saw Charlotte Satou. Alive. Please let her be alive. I didn't like Benjamin Satou. Robots and I don't mesh. Couldn't fully trust robotics. And it wasn't like it was just me. I had grounds. The hourly news blogs at home streamed scores of murders, accidental deaths and the like at the hands of some so-called friendly robot. Sure, friendly fire and fun funerals. Oxymorons.

Yeah, only morons trusted robots.

Coupled with human organic parts didn't temper that revulsion inside me. Lying had become a natural habit, but one thing I didn't do was lie to myself. Deception is best dealt from the deck and on to other game players, never to oneself.

"Pssst…" hissed a shadow seeping from out of a nearby pit. Covered in fluids, the person waved me over. Hands rested on narrowed hip and a bosom heaved.

I waited, feeling my heart increase it's thump-one, thump-two routine. Darn it, I missed my weapon. Without it I felt like I was running around nude. Confidence not withstanding, I inched closer, putting my hand into the satchel as if I had something dangerous.

"What?" I barked.

"You ain't a raider, so whatcha doin' here?" she asked, the voice had to be female, because the body obviously was. "Been watching you the last couple hours slink from one to the other."

"I'm looking for someone," I said, simple and to the point. A bit peeved that I stood out so well, I sighed. Could be that I didn't sport the jumpsuits or the ragtag clothing of the other scavengers.

"Everybody around here is dead. You can't see that?" she scoffed and crossed her arms over her chest. She had a satchel similar to mine on the ground at her feet. Items caused the bottom to bulge. "Good luck trying to find anything valuable in this. Dig for the older ones, they're easier to break."

Tick.

"I'll keep that in mind," I said, wishing I could wipe out the visual in my head her comments conjured. The soft whirling of a drive saving data gave me pause. "Ah, where are the latest ones anyway? The new stuff."

I'm referring to people as stuff. I need to get back home and be held.

"Why you want them? Harder. Rigor makes them rigid."

Tick.

I nodded and tried again to inquire nicely, where the latest batch of bodies resided.

"Pit or pile?" I asked and swept my arm outward.

The face behind the mask screwed up in thought.

"Can't be sure, but the one cargo craft got new updates yesterday," she explained and pointed to the west. "Now, see there's no one over by them, 'cuz no one but raiders grab the goodies. So, careful."

Tick.

"You're not a raider?" I asked, a bit surprised. Something about the woman rubbed my skin the wrong way. The strange ticking after each statement reminded me of Benjamin.

Satou.

Her head shook no so vehemently I thought it would zip off and land into one of the pits.

"Nuh uh," she scowled. "I'm a medical student at the Southwest Territories Academy for Medicine. I'm here doing research."

Tick.

Body snatcher.

Still a med student might prove more useful than say the raiders.

"About a week ago, the SE twilight sweep dropped off a ton of people, some not quite dead," I explained, inching closer, all of my suspicions blaring out a warning. "The woman I'm looking for might be in that group."

"A woman?" the med student scoffed, the scorn so heavy it escaped the sharp stripping of her mask.

Tick.

"Yeah," I laughed and shrugged, playing into the act we both were performing. "It seems they're a lot of women here, but it shouldn't be too hard to remember her. She was alive when she got here."

"What she look like?" she asked and wiped her hands on pants already well stained.

Tick.

I took out my handheld and called up the JPEG of Charlotte Satou. With a few more steps forward, I held it up for the woman. *Take a look and see what I got for you.*

"Her husband is sick with worry," I said, hoping the background would jostle something in the thin woman's memory or force her to confront that from which she had fled. She seemed very coherent considering she spent her time, a lot of it in this graveyard. "The soldier is a District infantryman home on leave."

"I have not seen her before," the woman turned away, voice falling flat. She got down on her knees and prepared to climb back down into the pit. "Leave."

"Sure?" I asked because all the body language confirmed the opposite. The change in voice cadence and tone sent a strange quiver through me. "Her husband needs her. Only love can help mend the horror of what he's seen and been through. A man needs his wife during a time like this."

"I do not remember her," the woman replied. *Tick.* "Leave." *Tick.*

"Charlotte," I said as the puzzle piece buzzing through my brain found a home. "Benjamin needs you."

She froze, hazel eyes burning like wheat on fire.

"What the hell are you doing here anyway?" I asked, not waiting for her confirmation. "Just spit it out. Tell me."

There. From beneath a fall of dripping and dirty braids, those eyes glowed with unrestrained fury spiraling outward so fast I felt it brush against me a second before she leapt from the ladder, sending it crashing to the ground. She lunged at me, hands at my throat. I saw it unfold in slow motion. Coldness filtered down my head to my feet like a glacier.

"Benjamin sent me to search for you," I said, fists in punching position.

With her hands inches from my throat, she froze. Eyes wide with disbelief and perhaps a touch of curiosity, she let out a nervous giggle.

That's when something Benjamin said clicked home. He said that Charlotte kept misspelling his name and each email sounded like a different person. I understood now why that happened.

Charlotte dropped her arms and heaved her satchel onto her shoulder. With a wave to come on, she marched off without a word. She stopped and waited while I caught up with her.

"Follow me."

Not speaking all the way to the EuroRepublic's barracks and bubble bioms, she flashed a badge and we drifted through the compound without issues.

My rabid curiosity was about to be fed.

But did I still want it?

THE END

CHARLOTTE SATOU'S sliver of living space took up a tiny six feet by five feet square. On the floor a mauve sleeping bag had been rolled up and shoved beneath the desk. A collapsed canvas chair rested against the soft bubble foam. A round bubble—talk about an oxymoron.

Like Charlotte Satou.

She stepped onto a patch of dark gray and as she did so, it warmed to a harsh scarlet. She unzipped the suit and it began to dissolve, melting the suit into the rectangular beneath her booted feet. Naked beneath the suit, she folded her arms across her chest. All the while, she avoided my direct gaze.

Modest?

I doubted it.

"You bring me here for a reason? I can't tell what time it is up here, but I'm sure at some point I should sleep."

"Yes, you should, if you can," Charlotte said in a whisper so faint it barely cleared the hum of the computer and electronics crammed onto her desk. "If your body will allow it."

Tick.

"I'm not here for the bio lesson," I snapped. "I'm here because your husband paid me to be."

At the mention of Benjamin, Charlotte closed her eyes.

"I can't go back to him now," she said, stepping off the box. She bent down, putting her back and its nudity to me. Naked or not, the woman presented a threat I couldn't look away from. With quick snatches and pulls, Charlotte had dressed in a space jacket and matching pants. The bottoms fit right over her boots. She hadn't needed to change them. They shone now they'd been cleaned of the muck.

The pad powered down to cool verdant as it processed the fluids and fabric of her bio-suit. She snatched the rubberband from her braids and shook them to free them further. As she did this, I saw it. The metallic glisten buried against the mass of licorice-like cords.

"Why not?" I asked, stepping backward, attempting to put distance between us. Benjamin knew, but he didn't care. "He loves you."

"Love isn't programmed into him, miss---"

"Lewis."

"Miss Lewis. Benjamin's only key emotion is fighting and immense hatred," she said, shrugging as she turned to face me. "He ordered you to find me because he needs maintenance. His four year rotation is up."

"Why are you here, Charlotte, on the EuroRepublic's base, working, scavenging for bodies, pretending to be a med student?" I asked, rotating my satchel's front flap around to stomach where I could dig into it for something to stop her if she snapped.

"Classified," she said, head tilting to the left.

"Your husband's life is threatened daily in the District's trenches and you, what? Scurry off to the enemy side for what purpose? Tell me. He needs to know."

She scoffed, flashing me a smile so fake I could bend it and reapply it on someone else.

"He needs maintenance."

"So, why come up here? Why not service him as your original orders had been programmed?"

Even if the purpose Benjamin sent me to find her was simply to locate her to fix his failing parts, I didn't care. I found her. I should leave, hop the next transport back to the District and consider the job finished.

But my curiosity rumbled in strong opposition.

"You know what I am?" she asked, eyebrows rising in surprise. "I am impressed, Miss Lewis."

"Your hair hides most of the cords, but not all. You're a cyborg, like him. Your transformation happened recently because a bunch of other people have been responding to your emails from Benjamin. When the DC Regulators came sniffing around, the Euros faked your correspondence. You didn't begin this way. I read your files, and your classification is human, non-engineered."

She grinned and it contained as much warmth as the one Benjamin gave.

"What do you do for them?"

"Classified."

She smiled again.

"If I guess correctly, you nod," I suggested, viewing her now as a computer program and not necessarily a person. "This way we can bypass your classified protocols. Deal?"

"Why would I do that?"

"Because Benjamin loves you," I said. "I know it's a crappy answer, but the truth isn't always polished and shiny. Part of him is still human, Charlotte and that piece of him needs that matching piece inside you."

"There are not any pieces of me that remain *human*," she said, and the absence of inflection, emotion, or empathy chilled me a bit. "I have not been programmed to love or to care."

The EuroRepublic. They snatched Charlotte Satou and transformed her into this, this piece of machinery. But why?

"Tell me about Benjamin Satou. Why did the District rework him into a cyborg?" I asked, attempting to work a different angle. Information about him wouldn't be classified.

"They took him because he almost died. The scientists had

taken over 1000 other gravely wounded soldiers before him. He was the first success. As test subject D1076, his body accepted the transplants, nanos, and robotics without constant rejection or other complications. I am test subject E0001..."

"That's enough," came the rumble from the bubble's open slit.

I whirled around, fists raised, but the familiarity of the voice set me on edge.

"Who the hell are you?" I asked, but as the person stepped into the light, my mouth went dry. "Benjamin?"

"Don't be silly, Miss Lewis," Benjamin laughed. "I am not here to fight, but thank you for finding my wife. Your payment is being progressed as we speak."

"I hadn't contacted you," I lowered my fists. "How'd you find me?"

"I have been here, tailing you since your arrival," he explained, but his eyes were all for Charlotte. "I have a stealth mode and night vision. Once activated, you wouldn't have smelled me, heard me, let alone seen me. It is the best feature, isn't it Char?"

She nodded. "Yes."

I stepped back from the chasm between them.

With their eyes locked on, she took a booted step toward him and lifted her fists. Her eyes, glowed to crimson bright, and with fists raised, body rigid in defensive mode, she said in an in-human voice, "E0001 has located target. Prepared for removal."

"HQ109, Benjamin here. I have located E0001. Engaging," Benjamin said, but with the tiniest hint of sadness.

Perhaps it was my imagination.

To my horror, Benjamin's eyes also glowed and his body moved in the sharp fighting position. He didn't look at me, but behind those scarlet orbs, I thought I saw shiny tears holding firm, refusing to fall.

He jerked like a rusty wauto as he stepped toward her. I inched along the edge of the bubble, ready to get the heck out of there. Two people who had once been in love had been transformed into bitter enemies. I hadn't picked a side in the war, but this interference into the lives of its soldiers had me more than annoyed with the EU.

Neither of them noticed me as I escaped into the bitter night.

Somehow reuniting two lovers didn't leave me feeling warm and fuzzy.

ABOUT THE AUTHOR

Nicole Givens Kurtz is the author of the futuristic thriller series, *Cybil Lewis*. Her novels have been named as finalists in the Fresh Voices in Science Fiction, EPPIE in Science Fiction, and Dream Realm Awards in science fiction. Nicole's short stories have earned an Honorable Mention in L. Ron Hubbard's Writers of the Future contest, and have appeared in such numerous anthologies and other publications.

Visit strange new worlds. Visit Other Worlds Pulp, Nicole's website, at http://www.nicolegivenskurtz.com or follow her on Twitter @nicolegkurtz.

WANT MORE CYBIL LEWIS